SKY DIAMONDS

Dawn's

Be aware
of your health
and keep
smiling —

Love, Doom
day.

8/24/2015

Sky Diamonds

the first of three books about the international adventures of Jim Gilchrist

Jim McGraw

ISBN 13:9781511979177

Library of Congress Registration Number: TXu 1-935-600
April 28, 2015   Washington, D.C.

Scriptural quotation is taken from the King James Version.

SKY DIAMONDS is a work of fiction,
and all of its characters are ficticious.
Any resemblance to actual events
or real persons, living or dead,
is entirely coincidental and unintentional.

Dedicated to

the United States Marine Corps,
the United States Navy Medical Corps,
the Fleet Marine Force,
and the Wounded Warrior Project

Acknowledgments

I would like to thank the following folks for
their contributions and encouragement:
Mrs. Dana McGraw, Mr. Mike Anderson, Mr. James Dubose III, Mr. Virgil Baker,
Dr. Barbara Jean Fant, Miss Eloise Penn, Mrs. Margaret Hearn,
Mrs. Chris Overton, Mr. and Mrs. Art and June Morrison, Mrs. Thurmond,
Mr. Bill Phinazee, Mr. and Mrs. Richard and Linda Shepherd, Coach S. C. Watkins,
Mrs. Betty Moore, Jonathan Johnson, Mrs. Azalean DeChau,
Mr. and Mrs. Ed and Vickie Noga, Mr. Chris Kennel, Mrs. Frankie Leather,
Mr. Joe Bradley, Mr. Stephen Davis, Mrs. Carolyn Brantley, Ms. Barbara
McClellan, Sgt. Blevins, Pfc. Don Sheppard, "Steamer", "O.D.",
Cpl. Donald France, Pfc. Bailey, Capt. "Buzz" Frye, "Sugar Bear", Cpl. Rogers,
Chief LaGranda, LCDr. Linda Adams, Mrs. Lo, Hm2 Jessie Patmore,
Lt. Linda Powell, Capt. Poucher, MDUSN,

and to my readers:

thank you so much for buying *SKY DIAMONDS*.
I look forward to entertaining you again with two more books about
the international adventures of Jim Gilchrist.

CONTENTS

AUTHOR'S INTRODUCTION

MANKIND HAS SEARCHED for the meaning of life for millenniums. The search has been called a race, a game, a journey, an adventure, and even a "box of chocolates" by poets, authors, journalists, and philosophers. My personal favorite is simply "to love and be loved." The pages of *SKY DIAMONDS*, the first book of a trilogy, unfurl my story as the character Jim Gilchrist, an extraordinary adventure of *joie de vivre* about delving into the meaning of life, exploring the globe via international travel, and thriving during episodes of joy, sorrow, dalliances, intrigue, and danger.

I extracted "the icing of life" that so few find.

Jim McGraw, 2015

"Rejoice, O young man, in thy youth; and let thy heart cheer thee in the days of thy youth..."

Ecclesiastes 11:9

1

[Jim humming: "The Shadow of Your Smile" by Frank Sinatra]

December 24, 1977

Dear Jim,

As always, when I write you, all our times together stream forth in my mind and bring me the happiest memories and the greatest love that anyone could have shared. My purpose in writing to you is to pray you will come back to England very soon and see our son, David, who is seven. I am married now to a fine gentleman who supports David and me in grand fashion. His name is Jake Samples, and he's an administrative officer with the U.S. Embassy here in London. You would like him and the lifestyle he has provided for both David and me.

Your letters to me and what we have shared are still precious to me, and I often read your letters over and over and remember the few magical years we spent together. David is you almost in total. He has your crystal-blue eyes, your olive-toned skin, and your lush brown hair. He is cu-rious about every aspect of life, and his incredible imagi-nation and sense of humor remind me of you every day. Your trips over to London to visit me in the early '70s are still some of my happiest memories; seeing David as a child made us both smile with delight. I know you strug-gled to leave us behind as he aged and became used to you and your warmth for both of us. Even in his early years, David sensed we were very special to each other.

Anyway, please write to me again at the old post-of-fice box we have used over the past seven years, which no one else knows about ... it is still my secret place of joy to visit. We now live out in Bromley, which you are very familiar with. The Ramblers Rest, your favorite pub, is still there, and they still hang your private beer stein on the wall, awaiting your return, as do I.

Loving you still,

Jill

P.S. Non-stop snow here in London since your Thanksgiv-ing!

January 1, 1978

Dearest Jill,

I never tire of your letters. Yes, those frequent visits to you and our son, David, in London in the early '70s are still deep in my mind and memories ... perhaps the happiest ones of my life too. You've always reminded me of our age difference, but I think we both know it has made little to no difference in our relationship. When we first met, you were a mere girl even at forty, and I was at least well-traveled, thanks to the Marines, and worldly by twenty-three. The difference in our ages never crossed my mind then or now.

Yes, I would love to visit you both in London when I finish this season's luxury charters with Pan American. I will have all of March and April off to catch up on my personal travel after months of transporting tourists throughout Western Europe. Let me know some dates that you can manage without interfering with your medical consulting assignments for the private hospitals in the British Isles. I would think that between your expensive fees and your husband's salary at London's U.S. Embassy, you should be doing quite well and in the dough. I am enjoying a luxurious life, flying first class, and staying in five-star luxury hotels, all on my meager charter-rep salary! Yes, Pan American Airlines does "make the going great" for a divorced bachelor employee like me. I'm still a travel whore.

I will make sure to stop over in London on my way to the French countryside, the Amalfi coast, and my favorite retreat at Lake Como, Italy. Wish you could join me, even bringing Jake and David. I could be "Uncle Jim" from San Francisco. The travel wholesalers have offered to treat me and to pick up all my expenses, including a small villa in my favorite places, a car and driver, and my food and booze.

Your loving Fleet Marine Corpsman,

Jim

P.S. I remember our walking in the snow in London with David on my back when he was just a baby.

2

[JIM HUMMING: "WHO CAN I TURN TO WHEN NOBODY NEEDS ME?" BY TONY BENNETT]

Danang Air Terminal, Vietnam
Medevac Flights to Yokosuka Naval Hospital, Japan
July 1969

THE VIETNAMESE WAR was harrowing in every way. My wounds were minor compared to the jarheads who were severely wounded during an ambush we encountered near firebase Stud (a.k.a. firebase Vandergriff). I was wounded in the right forearm with mortar blasts and shrapnel. While these were not severe wounds, the danger was to the nerves in my right forearm, which could possibly cause me a form of paralysis and a dragging right arm. The surgeons who specialized in this type of wound were world renowned and were from Switzerland and Germany, but during the war, they donated their time to serve at the Naval Hospital in Yokosuka, Japan.

I was tripping on morphine drips and the smell of Shalimar perfume from the gorgeous Navy nurses who helped load us into the giant aircraft provided by Braniff Airlines (Lady Bird Johnson's private boondoggle) for our four hour flight from Vietnam to Yokosuka, Japan. I slept much of the journey but still was enjoying the soothing touches and the familiar fragrances of my American "round-eyed" nurses. Any female with round eyes was beautiful to me now. After eating and sleeping in the mud of the Vietnamese jungle, I treasured these clean new surroundings as heaven on Earth.

When I arrived at check-in at the Yokosuka Naval Hospital in Japan, I was immediately taken to the surgical ward on the sixth floor, where another team of nurses awaited our arrival and checked us into the system. My wound was evaluated again, and a pretty brunette nurse from Montana applied a new dressing. She was fastidious in her cleaning of the wound and re-dressing the old bandage. She asked if my pain was severe, and when I answered in the affirmative, she started a morphine drip. I felt no more pain.

I must have slept most of the night, and as I awoke to the bright lights and stark noises from the hospital staff, I heard "Reveille." Everyone who could possibly sit up or hobble up to a stance stood for that, and a very welcomed hot American breakfast was served at 0700. Clean sheets, showers, soft pillows, and beautifully shaped nurses were a feast for the senses. I was happy for a short time just being out of the war and away from flying bullets, but then the morphine started wearing off. Creeping back into my mind came the unwanted memories of home, a destroyed mar-riage, and the unfaithfulness of my wife.

The charge nurse cheerfully approached us after breakfast to make sure we contacted our loved ones back home via phone or if the trooper's family had no phone, by written letter, which was commonplace among the lower-income Marines. The common young Marine had a modest high-school education and was usually from a poor rural or urban area, like the coal-mining towns of West Virginia or the cattle country in Texas or Oklahoma. Many had dropped out of high school and lied about their ages to get into the Marine Corps; their real ages were commonly in the mid- to late teens. Many of the Marines had their first new pair of boots and new clothes, and with seventy-eight dollars' monthly pay, they also had their first taste of independence. Most were so poor that they had survived on hand-me-down shoes and clothes just so they could work or farm. Many were orphans, and some already had served jail time for fighting or drunkenness. A goodly number of them were given the choice of jail time or enlisting in the Marine Corps. The choice was a foregone conclusion. The corps had done a pretty good job of squaring them away—cleaning up their lives physically and mentally to do one task: search and destroy. They were excellent troopers. Each one of them was a hell of a good fighter, and they loved being drunk when not in the bush.

The head ward nurse approached me and asked who I wanted to call. She noticed that my records indicated I was married with one child and also had my parents listed as contacts.

"Would you like to call your wife and let her know your status?"

I laughed and said, "No, my estranged wife has already taken up with an Army guy back home in Atlanta!"

She politely asked if I'd like to talk to my mom and dad, and I gave her a grateful affirmative answer. I was helped into a wheelchair and taken to a telecom room where I had a booth for privacy. The nurse dialed the number at my folks' house, and my mom answered the phone with great anticipation and tearful joy.

"How are you?!" she shouted. It was 4:00 a.m. there, and she had already heard from the Red Cross that I had been wounded, and she had been worried sick about the severity of the wounds. I calmed her down and assured her that my wounds were now minor and could be taken care of in a couple of weeks or so. Dad took the receiver from Mom and asked if I was resting and getting some good American food yet. I answered him that we'd been getting three cold beers a day, all the food we could eat, lots of pretty nurses, and lots of rest. We chatted small talk for several minutes, until my time was almost up. Mom came back on the phone and asked if I had called my estranged wife, Jenny, yet.

I answered, "No! Enough has been said between us already, and I'm resigned to a divorce by proxy."

Jenny had shacked up with *him* and was already taking my young daughter, Susan Michelle, to see *his* parents, as though I was no longer her father. I was relieved to be through with the marriage. We had married so young, and both of us had changed greatly over the past three years. A brief and awkward two weeks off duty for rest and relaxation in 1968 in Hawaii had been the swan song to our marriage.

Returning me to the ward, the head nurse indicated that it was my turn to be interviewed by the Chief of Surgery, Dr. Jill Meadows. The nurse indicated that this final interview was part of the triage process, after we had been screened by the nursing staff who actually changed our dressings, fed us, and took care of all our cleaning procedures. When I asked her what the head Doc was like, she smiled and said she was very stern and forthright in her evaluation of each surgical patient. The nurse commented that Dr. Jill Meadows was also beautiful and had a great sense of humor. I was curious and somewhat nervous to be interviewed by a Navy Captain. I expected an older, white-haired doctor with age spots and a nasty disposition toward Marines. Perhaps she would give me a break since I had been a Navy Fleet Marine Corpsman myself!

The interview was scheduled for the next morning at ten o'clock in the doctor's office in Japan. After breakfast and changed dressings, I arrived in Capt. Jill Meadows's large office overlooking the base at Yokosuka Naval Hospital, Japan. The office was empty for about ten minutes, and then she made her entrance. I was stunned by her beauty and how young she looked. She smiled and asked if I had been given good nursing care and medical treatment.

I answered, "Yes, the very best care that could be given."

She was delighted to hear that. She stated that she was to give me an overall picture of what I was facing surgically and how long I would probably stay at the hospital. She said I would have an exploratory surgery followed by a repair surgery to fix the nerve damage in my right arm. She indicated that I would probably have an additional follow-up surgery in the Balboa Naval Hospital in San Diego to make the lasting adjustments to the nerves and that the surgery would be performed by experts in surgical nerve damage. She said I would not return to the Fourth Marines, since the damage was severe enough to relieve me of my field-medical duties.

"This is your ticket home, Corpsman," she stated reassuringly.

I still was awestruck by her easy charm and beauty. She looked thirtyish, but I found out later she was actually forty. The meeting was more than cordial and informative, and I was pleased not to find her the usual stern authoritative Navy Captain I had been expecting. For a long time after she left, I remained still, enjoying my lingering thoughts of her beautiful shape until I was escorted back to my room.

3

[JIM HUMMING: "WE GOTTA GET OUTTA THIS
PLACE" BY ERIC BURDON & THE ANIMALS]

WHILE AWAITING SURGERY, I read and listened to the latest music played on the cassette players bought by those Marines who had almost completed their surgical procedures. On our ward we had a ward attendant who oversaw the bed linens, towels, and wash clothes. His name was Mr. Lunoloe, a Filipino with a wicked sense of humor who was merciless to the Marine patients who had reached the point of recovery so that they were complaining about either going back home or returning to "the Nam." Mr. Lunoloe ran a tight ship and saw to it that the bed linens were changed daily either by the lower-ranking nurses or in some cases the patients themselves. He often cussed at us about how spoiled we were to have beautiful nurses, cold beer, great food, and entertainment. His verbiage was "salty" at best, and the nurses blushed at his language.

One day I challenged him on his life in the Philippines and asked him what he did in his village that was so different from our way of life. He answered loud enough for the whole ward to hear, "Well, we fuck all day, and all night we fucking and more fucking till we all fucked out. You fucking Marines don't know how to fuck and please your women."

He stated that he had four wives and too many girlfriends to count. The nurses blushed to hear his racy diatribe, and the senior ward nurse, Commander Sears, had reprimanded him more than a few times. The ward was rolling in laughter, and all the patients told and retold with snickers Lunoloe's idea of the plight of the poor sex life of a Marine. I found it curious that the Japanese employees looked down on the Filipinos as "Asian niggers" or half-breeds with Spanish blood. Racial prejudice has no boundaries around the world.

The time for my surgery came, and it went well. I remember the surgeons speaking in both German and English. They had volunteered their time and their skills in order to bring over their understudies so they could experience trauma wounds from war and the new techniques developed to be used on soldiers. My surgery took four hours due to the damage inflicted by the shrapnel and the blast from an RPG (rocket-propelled grenade). Then it took two additional hours to recover from the anesthesia, which had put me into my first deep, restful sleep since Nam, the first sleep deep enough that I was not interrupted by episodes of PTSD (post-traumatic stress disorder).

I had some pain when I awoke, but the morphine drip was helping. I slept on and off for several days before they got me up and moved me around to avoid pneumonia and other possible complications from the surgery. One of the nurses said that the top Navy surgeon, Capt. Jill Meadows, had come by to check on me and had sat next to my bed attentively for over an hour—an unusually long time given her modus operandi and hectic schedule. From what the nurses said, she had never done that before. I learned later that Captain Meadows had been married to a Navy Fleet Marine Corpsman who had been killed in action several years earlier, and she carried a lingering soft spot in her heart for field medical corpsmen and the job they did for the Marines in their care.

I recovered quickly and was up and about in several days, having only minor pain in my right arm. The painkillers were almost an addiction for me at this point. Nurse Commander Sears stated that I would be given recovery leave while in Japan for a week or so and that the second surgery would be either here or in San Diego. I was excited about seeing Japan on my convalescent leave.

Cpt. Jill Meadows came by on several more occasions to check on my recovery and to give me some great ideas on what to visit while touring Japan on my leave. She placed great emphasis on Kyoto and stated that it was her favorite destination of all the cities in Japan to visit. Along with these tidbits of travel information, she gave me the name of her favorite hotel in Kyoto. There was a connection between us that I felt but could not completely understand. We were both interested in each other and had many questions to be asked away from the hospital. It was a tenuous feeling of mutual curiosity and physical attraction.

I planned my trip and had the transportation officer arrange my train ride and make my hotel reservations at the beautiful spot Jill had mentioned just outside Kyoto. When I arrived, the flower fragrances swept me out of reality. The hotel was surrounded by flowers and rock gardens that nostalgically brought me back to a sense of serenity and composure I had not felt in years. The garden was romantic and filled with a quiet reverence for the Creator. My room was simple but did have a Western queen-size bed, an abundance of the freshest flowers, and sake wine. I felt truly at peace for the first time since before the war and felt my soul finally sigh as I breathed out. My mind began to wander.

Daydreams so rarely come true, but mine would.

I had arrived at my hotel around noon and had lunch in the tea garden café next to the rock garden. I wanted a non-tea drink afterwards and adjourned to a small bar that had a tiny fireplace and was filled with Japanese locals. As I was seated, a hand gently touched my back and slid down my arm. It was Cpt. Jill Meadows. I smiled a sheepish grin and took her hand as we moved to a table near the small fireplace.

Even though I was delighted to see her, I sensed that the rendezvous was not entirely accidental. The lowly transportation officer who had made my reservations would have been more than willing to divulge my travel itinerary had the beautiful Captain Meadows inquired. She asked if I was surprised to see her. I said delightfully surprised, and the tea garden now felt transformed into a private paradise just by her presence. She said she had so many questions about my life, and I returned with a curious interest in her own life. We talked on for hours and hours, until it was obvious that we were both intimately interested in the tales of each other's unusual and extraordinary life. I think I fell in love with her mind as I watched her and listened to her tales, but it was confirmed when she smiled at me and took my hand to hold. Her gentle touch warmed all our conversations, and I began to feel that she was gradually reciprocating the same feelings that I had of an unusual convergence of souls.

We talked intimately, holding hands, and staring into each other's eyes, for several more hours, which seemed to pass like a few seconds in time. We shared family backgrounds and stories about our schools and travels. She confided in me that she

intended to take an early twenty-year retirement once her transfer to San Diego was approved. At twenty-three I was somewhat
surprised that she could take full retirement at forty years old as
a Navy Captain. She squeezed my hand in hers, and we continued
to stare at each other. It was edgy. We both shared smiles and the
knowledge that something special was beginning to happen.

Jill had taken the room next to mine, knowing the hotel well
from her numerous visits in the past. While still at our table, she
told me that I was the first man she had wanted to be with in over
two years, since her husband had died in combat. The air was
electric with passion and desire and just plain wanting someone
who was living and healthy to hold on to. We walked slowly to
her room, which was a large, open room with a queen-size bed
and small fireplace. The fire was already lit and flickering. The air
outside was somewhat chilly and damp, but the fire inside gave a
warming welcome to two friends in this strange and exotic place.

Upon opening her door and leading her inside, I immediately
took her in my arms and held her against the back of the closed
door, kissing her mouth hard and deeply. She responded immediately with great passion and desire and then melted in my arms to
be taken. I placed my hands around her and lifted her skirt up so
I could reach my hands into her panties and pull them away from
the soft, warm flesh of her hips. She pressed herself tightly against
me, and I knew she could feel how hard and ready I was for her.

We continued to kiss as I undressed her and she undressed
me. We fell to the floor in the nude and made out passionately for
several minutes. I turned her on her back, and she lifted her legs
into the air, spreading them as I moved in between them. She let
out a small scream and then moaned softy as I banged her over and
over again. We both came and stilled and sighed. Once recovered,
we walked eagerly over to the bed, anxious now to repeat the acts

of intimacy over and over in different positions. It was hot and magical—the best sex I had ever had. She thanked me for being *the man* she had passionately wanted.

The following week we visited the sights of Kyoto and surrounding environs, and we were both happy and at peace with our newfound relationship. We spent hours talking about our youth, families, and experiences of life in general. We smiled constantly and felt free from the lives we had left behind, if only for a short week. Knowingly Jill had brought medical supplies to change my dressings, even though the wound was mostly closed and healing well. She was my angel on Earth, with long, swaying strawberry-blond hair, sparkling-blue eyes, and long, knockout legs that seemed to run all the way to her neck. She turned heads wherever we went. I never felt jealous when the other troopers stared at her, knowing that she was mine…at least for now…and maybe much longer. What a joyous feeling to be in love again, albeit a love with an uncertain future.

4

[JIM HUMMING: "WINDY" BY

THE ASSOCIATION]

JILL RETURNED TO the hospital in Yokosuka, Japan, several days before I returned to be checked out. This helped us cover any questions others may have asked about our coinciding absences from the surgical ward. These few days of separation from Jill also let me ponder where I would go and what I would do upon my discharge, which was only a few months away now. Jill indicated that she would have me released about the same time that she would transfer to the San Diego Naval Hospital.

To coordinate with my recovery from my final surgery and release from the San Diego Naval Hospital, Jill had scheduled on the same day her formal departure appointment, which was loaded with paperwork. The US Navy would give a formal retirement party for her that same evening in San Diego. We discussed my attendance as her escort but decided it might prick unwelcome and/ or judgmental comments from the senior medical officers there, some of whom had had strong crushes on Cpt. Jill Meadows since her husband had been killed two years earlier. She was a prize catch in their eyes, as she was in mine. I felt we had a strong future together, even if we had been parted for much of our lives.

We discussed the separations due to our jobs while in Kyoto and agreed that both our futures would probably require international travel from time to time. Jill had already received several tremendous job offers both as a surgical consultant and as a medical administrator. We both agreed that San Francisco would be our common base of operation. I had already written Pan American Airways, hoping to land a spot as a charter salesman out of San Francisco. It wasn't much of a salary, but the incredible travel benefits and the two months off each year made up for any difference. Jill and I both discussed our choices as to where to settle in the San Francisco area and where to make a nest for ourselves between trips. We both wanted to be near the San Francisco airport, and our plans would include taking as many trips together as possible.

Captain Meadows had arranged for us to leave Japan for San Diego on the same flight. We flew a Pan Am jet to San Fran, where we made the shorter flight on to San Diego. At the Balboa Naval Hospital, Dr. Jill Meadows was busy finishing her time out until her retirement day. I was laid up in the surgical ward, recovering from nerve damage and surgery. We shared smiles and winks whenever possible. I watched other senior medical staff and doctors alike constantly pursue her, but she kindly denied them all. I continued to burn for her, and from her looks back at me, the feeling was mutual.

By September 1969 I had one more minor surgery to be scheduled at the Balboa Naval Hospital in San Diego to complete the repair of the nerve damage done to my arm in Nam. I recovered quickly from the surgery but was bedridden and caught sight of

Jill only from time to time. With a myriad number of military women and airline stewardesses who were needy and forward, even offering to be at my beck and call, I was only on fire for Jill.

Cpt. Jill Meadows's retirement ceremony at the Balboa Naval Hospital in San Diego was grand and beautiful and filled with great stories and remembrances of her outstanding service. Well over two hundred Navy folk and civilians attended the ceremony. I watched from the balcony near the hospital gardens. Jill received numerous accolades and praises from the staff and especially from a female Navy Admiral with whom she had performed years of surgical procedures. Jill received a beautiful and expensive ring to commemorate her twenty years of service. The ring was solid gold with over two carats of tiny diamonds in the shape of a Navy anchor and globe. She was overwhelmed and had tears of joy reliving old memories with the best of her Navy friends.

My discharge was scheduled for one week after the retirement party. Jill went on a week ahead of me to San Francisco to look at possible houses for us. I joined her at the Top of the Mark Hotel, where she had a wonderful room with a view overlooking the bay. We made frantic love until evening and then had dinner at The Mark with lots of bourbons chased with beer, along with a perfect chef's choice steak, which we shared. We were both sloshed and pleasantly full. The next step was bed again. We made love all evening and returned to the bar around midnight, where the nightly festivities were continuing. We danced to Ramsey Lewis and his rendition of "The In-Crowd" and "Sunday in Memphis."

The next day we went shopping for houses together. Jill and I decided on the Walnut Creek area across the bay for our nest between our business travels. We found a small, two-bedroom cottage with a beautiful gazebo, garden, fireplace, and sun room, which was already filled with plants. I had not been this happy in years, and Jill was joyous and anxious for us to begin our careers and travels. I was a kept man for several weeks until Pan American finally completed the paperwork, and I was officially hired to sell the jet and land luxury-charter arrangements for companies in the Western United States. The salary was only $22,000 per year plus a commission for any incentive charters I would sell.

Jill, on the other hand, had accumulated quite a nest egg. She had her savings from her twenty years in the Navy plus signing bonuses and the death benefits from her late husband. She had landed a consulting position with the International Medical Corps, making over $ 60,000 a year including all first-class travel and accommodations. Jill was ecstatic and playfully rubbed it in about the vast difference in our salaries. She did admit that she wouldn't have the two months off per year and the thousands of dollars I would surely receive in commissions and gratis travel benefits provided to the network of tour operators, which could possibly total her base salary. We were overjoyed with the luck we had with our careers.

After years in the military and being accustomed to the rigorous demands of the Navy, Jill and I treasured every second of our weeklong honeymooning and celebrated with pure joy our newfound freedom, good fortune, and happiness. It was heaven on Earth, but we had yet to receive our travel itineraries from our employers. When the itineraries both arrived, we were saddened a bit, noticing that we would be apart sometimes for weeks. I was immediately inundated with sales requests to set up charters for the early spring in Western Europe, including the month of May. I sold, planned, and set up charters and land arrangements for Transamerica, Boeing, and numerous other Fortune 500 companies.

After several weeks of our new career routines, I reopened the question of what I should do about my daughter back in Atlanta. Jill encouraged me to seek professional help dealing with the unthinkable adoption that my ex-wife had demanded and with any future relationship that might evolve with Susan Michelle. The next week I contacted the best shrink in San Francisco, Dr. Nancy Stein, who specialized in working with the individual parents during the adoption process of children from divorced couples. I was to leave on Friday for my first charter with Pan American and saw Dr. Stein on Wednesday before my trip. We talked for two days in a two-hour session each day.

I learned volumes from Dr. Stein, but the knowledge gave me a mountain of considerations as well as a great fretful sadness even to think about making a decision that would affect Susan Michelle's life for decades to come. It was by far the hardest and most difficult decision I had ever had to make in my life. I grieved uncontrollably as Jill and I reviewed the advice and conclusions from Dr. Stein, and we both wept. Under the circumstances, with my ex-wife marrying her shack-up Army guy, I had been threatened by her that Susan Michelle would be separated not only from me but also from my mom and dad, who had raised her during my Nam assignment. My ex-wife regarded my family as rednecks and said she would do everything she could to separate Susan Michelle from all of us.

This agonizing situation would cause decades of sorrow and sadness for my mom, dad, and me. The only singular advantage in my decision, Dr. Stein mentioned to me repeatedly, was for Susan. If I did decide to allow my ex-wife and her husband to adopt Susan, I was giving Susan Michelle, who was only two now, the only peace and security I could give her. At two she would barely remember me from our scant family time in Hawaii over a year ago. Susan Michelle's new life would be free from the friction and despair caused by visitation hassles and by the wrath of my ex-wife's insidious plan to displace Susan from my mom and dad, who had loved her so while I was away. I pushed the heartbreaking decision on the question of her adoption off until after I returned from Europe. I just needed more time to think about losing the true tiny love of my life.

Pan American had scheduled the first four luxury charters that I had sold. I would be splitting the top executives onto two Boeing 707s and arranging for the other employees to travel over on separate jets, all leaving San Francisco together. It was my full responsibility to entertain the top execs and make the trip a memorable one for all parties.

The trips to London included the Lake Country and the Cotswolds. I had established a good working relationship with the CEO of Transamerica, and he knew I was to stay only a few days with them on their ten-day excursion. After several days I boarded a "dead head"—an empty 707 returning from London back to San Francisco. I was totally preoccupied with the crushing emotional conundrum regarding the decision I had to make about Susan Michelle's adoption and with trying to maintain rights to a relationship with her as her *real* father. As always I was plagued with nausea and sleeplessness over the inevitable impending decision. Several of the stews on the dead-head flight offered me Dramamine for my sickness. It had little or no effect on the problem, which originated in my troubled mind.

Jill met me at the airport and tried futilely to comfort me after the long polar flight. We drove on home in silence in the late evening to our little nest in Walnut Creek. We were both somber, thinking about the abhorrent adoption decision ahead for me but didn't discuss it until we got home and had several stiff drinks. Finally breaking the silence, I told Jill I had made a decision about the adoption. I said it slowly, with my teeth gritted, but neither of us will like it. I went into great detail about my decision to allow them to adopt Susan according to the stern advice Dr. Stein had repeatedly given to me. I had wanted to attempt being an extended father to Susan, but Dr. Stein had strongly convinced me against that. If I even attempted to be a bicoastal absentee dad, the strain of arranging visits and the anguish on each departure would crush Susan Michelle.

The anticipated legal harangue that my ex-wife would instigate to restrain Susan from seeing me, my mom, and my dad, along with the stress on all of us, would be an unimaginable nightmare for Susan Michelle to go through. Dr. Stein said sternly to me over and over that the *best* thing I could do for Susan's sake was to allow them to adopt her, and when she became a young woman, she would probably seek me out, and we could then enjoy a father-daughter relationship. The adoption would make moot all the hellish times of travel separations, legal fights, stress, and confusion for Susan Michelle. Also, I cringed knowing that my ex-wife would create extra chaos at every opportunity in Susan's life and blame it on me.

I resigned myself to the decision, and even Jill eventually accepted my decision and seemed to understand more of Dr. Stein's reasoning than I expected. We slept finally after that long, long night. Out of tremendous love for my daughter, I had finally chosen a course, right or wrong but a course that I was now convinced was the only one I could make as a loving father in the best interest of my daughter, Susan Michelle.

Neither of us had even felt like eating dinner the night before, and our breakfast the next morning was hardy. We left for Zack's by the Bay, facing the waterfront near Sausalito. We ordered our favorites—eggs Benedict and champagne along with strawberry ice cream and coffee with Frangelico. We held hands and were resigned to the gut-wrenching decision I had had to make over the past several months. So much had transpired since the Navy hospital in Yokosuka, Japan. We both shared a sense of purpose and enthusiasm over the coming challenges of our careers. We faced our unknown futures as children of the world on a vast new adventure. Even though I was twenty-three now, and she was forty, I loved Jill more than ever. We had not discussed *her* own desire for a child or even if it would be a viable possibility at her age.

5

[JIM HUMMING: "LIL' GTO" BY

RONNY & THE DAYTONAS]

JILL WAS WELL received at the International Medical Corps. Her new job was headquartered in San Francisco, and she impressed the brass straightaway. She also received her first travel assignment, working with a large hospital in Seattle. The administration wanted to meet the gal who had already helped them so much via phone and telex. Jill planned her trip on a Friday afternoon so we could have time together in Seattle. We landed in Seattle to a rare occurrence—the cleanest deep-blue skies, clear of any clouds or chance of rain.

We checked into the Ritz-Carlton, had a wonderful dinner, and discussed our two days to play after our several weeks of hectic work schedules. I had done some research on the sights in the area. There was time to ferry over to Victoria in British Columbia, Canada, and return via Anacortes, a little village in the San Juan Isles on the Puget Sound in the state of Washington. The village of Anacortes was highly regarded by locals and nationals alike. After an early morning ferry ride over to Victoria, we explored the world-renowned Butchart Gardens all of Saturday morning. We took tea at the equally impressive Empress of China Hotel, rented a car, and took the ferry over to Anacortes late that evening. We chose a bed and breakfast called the Sea Wren, overlooking Puget Sound. We always tried to choose a room with a fireplace and found a small Victorian suite true to our desire. It had king-size bed, a fireplace, and several overstuffed chairs for total comfort. The smell of fresh flowers filled the room with an old-world, romantic fragrance. The radio was playing Etta James singing "At Last" while we danced slowly in our private little suite. I kissed Jill's neck gently and led her to bed. We made love passionately well into the early morning with only brief naps in between.

Saturday morning we drove all over Anacortes. The sky was as clear as a bell, just like the sky that had greeted us when we'd arrived in Seattle. Our rental car, a 1969 Pontiac Firebird, made the going great, and we cruised through the village and the surrounding parks and orchards. We ate lunch at a quaint little cafe on the pier, named the Captain's Retreat. I asked Jill what she would like to do before driving south back to Seattle that evening. She said she wanted to look at small cottages, being so overwhelmed with Anacortes and the beauty that surrounded it, the ocean, the sea smells, and shore birds on wing all around us. She shocked me when she said she would definitely have a house there someday. I jokingly asked if I would be included, and she replied that the cottage she would buy would always be there for both of us.

We picked up several brochures on the local houses for sale in Anacortes. The prices were relatively inexpensive considering the beauty of this little piece of heaven. We drove to several of the properties, if for no other reason than just to dream and wonder about having a cozy getaway from the pressures of our jobs and the demands made on our everyday lives. We laughed and listened to the car radio. The Beach Boys were singing "California Girls," and the Beatles were singing "She Loves You" a little too loudly; we probably disturbed the peace just riding around in several neighborhoods. Jill joked that I was still a kid at heart, only being twenty-three to her forty.

We drove back to Seattle and settled into the hotel around eight o'clock at night, exhausted but feeling great. I had an early bird flight on Pacific SW Airlines back to San Francisco at 6:30 a.m. Jill was to meet with her client the next morning at nine. I woke her around five and kissed her good-bye, and she fell back to sleep.

My flight back to San Francisco was intriguing. I flew on my first-class airline pass. There was a beautiful redheaded stewardess in first class who showed me great service and an unusual amount of personal attention. Her eyes were a beautiful gray, so I assumed she was Greek or Syrian. Once we were up in the air, she settled in right next to my window seat. Flirt! The flight was almost empty that time of morning. We discussed our positions with our respective airlines; she admired the Pan Am men and regal reputation of the airline. She boldly asked if I was married, and I honestly indicated to her that not only was I in the process of divorcing an estranged wife back in Atlanta, but also I was becoming quite involved with a special girl in San Francisco. Her unusual interest in me seemed to peak even more after I revealed a little personal information. She snuggled up even closer to me and brushed her right breast against my left arm; her beautiful, flowing red locks were splayed possessively all over me. I was surprised but felt twenty again quickly; she looked early twenties herself. She expertly stroked my ego, and I loved it, but I didn't see her doing that with any of the other passengers.

Melina insisted that I take her card with her private number and beguilingly pleaded that if my "special girl in San Fran" ever let me down to please, please, please call her. As we landed she flirtingly said with a final sweep of her red locks that she hoped very much to see me again, at least on future coastal flights.

Jill spent the week in Seattle and returned to San Francisco on Friday evening.

During that week I had a ball picking out a car for us to use in our home nest area around Walnut Creek and San Francisco. I was set on finding a used Pontiac GTO and looked at several different years. The final choice was a 1967 GTO with a 389 engine, tri power, Hurst close-ratio four-speed, and positraction rear end. My twenty-three years loved that it was also a candy-apple-red convertible. I took her for many spins and surprised Jill with it at the airport when I picked her up from her Seattle business trip.

Jill loved the fact that we now had our own car to use around Walnut Creek but raised her eyebrows at the color. Jill was looking at *my* car with her forty-year-old eyes—the first and only time our age difference had ever shown! Jill finally giggled that I had picked out a candy-apple-red car for us. We hugged and kissed with instant passion for each other and sheer thankfulness to be together again.

Jill did love that the GTO was a convertible, and we enjoyed the cool evening breezes across the bay on the drive home to Walnut Creek. While I was driving, Jill suddenly became quiet and thoughtful and stated that she had two very serious issues to discuss over dinner. A little bit anxious to hear the topics, I quickly pulled into the old Cliff House Restaurant for dinner and found a remote, private table away from the busy dinner clientele. I was on fire to know what had elicited this serious side to Jill. I had never seen her quite this serious, even during some of our more intimate conversations.

First she said slowly that she had bought outright with cash the cute little cottage with the beautiful gardens in Anacortes that we had looked at and had bought it at a great bargain! I was flushed with delight yet shocked and overwhelmed at her mature business savvy at the same time. After toasting the purchase, we had a light dinner of fresh salmon and wilted spinach salad. Now, what on Earth could be the second profound issue she was waiting all the way through dinner to tell me?

"I'm pregnant," she finally announced ecstatically. I was so shocked and startled, I could hardly breathe or swallow. She held back for a long time and then released a giggly smile after I caught my breath. "Are you happy?" she queried teasingly.

"Why, yes. Mostly surprised but happy for you at the same time."

We discussed due dates and all the doctors she wanted me to research and interview in San Fran to be her ob-gyn. Jill made it very clear that she did not expect us to marry and that I would have no obligations whatsoever to the child. No financial obligations at all…period. At twenty-three, temporarily, I felt used; my hands began to sweat, but finally my breathing returned to normal again. Jill said cheerfully that it was the happiest she had ever been and that she wanted a baby boy.

Recovering a little of my demeanor after Jill repeated slowly several more times for me that she really expected nothing else from me regarding the child, I was still stunned and lost in my own flood of thoughts about Susan Michelle. Finally I was able to speak somewhat normally again, and I asked her how she had found out. Jill said she had had a physical in San Francisco, required for her new job, and discovered the news when her test results came back.

I was immediately concerned about her future career with her new employer, since she had become pregnant so soon after being hired. I asked about her job, and she stated that they were delighted for her and wanted her to work as long as she pleased, even pregnant. Now I was happy and pleased for her, knowing her professional career was intact and her natural desire for a child would complete her as a woman. It turned out to be a magical evening as we drove back to Walnut Creek. I was ecstatically happy just thinking about *my* baby, the GTO, of course, and Jill was happy thinking about her own baby. Now life was good for both of us.

The Atlanta lawyers worked out all the details and finalized my wanted divorce and the unwanted adoption of no-longer-my-daughter Susan Michelle; her new last name would be Cutler. I felt sad that the awful, gut-wrenching adoption decision had now become a painful reality. Jill tried futilely to cheer me up with a double Maker's Mark and beer. We snuggled next to each other in front of the patio fireplace, wearing sweaters to keep the evening chill at bay. I would have felt cold anyway. The adoption was final, but my heart would always belong to Susan Michelle.

The next morning we left for work and began our careers in earnest. Now at least we'd have some semblance of a routine even though our travels would frequently interfere with our cherished love life. Now that the midwinter season for charters had ended, I began the grunt work of selling the future plane and land arrangements to the Fortune 500 companies across the Western United States. I birddogged every company I could think of that would be interested in incentive charters. The incentive charter is exactly what it says. For example, if you sell three hundred stoves or TVs, you get a free trip to Europe, all expenses paid, all on the company's dime.

In addition to selling the charter-plane reservations, I was responsible for all the land arrangements: hotels, meals, sightseeing, tours, tour guides, motor coaches, shopping side trips, etc. It was a hectic routine to plan from June through October. Pan Am even wanted me to fill the planes during the winter months, to cover the cost of fuel and payroll, so I was often furloughing many of the stews and ground crews. I would often accompany the chief executives on the first plane over to our mostly European destinations and then return on a dead-head flight, with the seats stacked high with large mailbags to help recover some of the cost of the flight's crew and fuel. The salary was still not much, but the commissions and perks were increasingly good, and I was going to have March and April off completely.

6

January 3, 1970

Dear Jim [via telex],

I am so excited about the baby, and my job is terrific. The company has been overly generous with salary, benefits, and time for me to rest and relax. How do you like Munich? I know this is a particularly important group of charters for you and pray you are satisfied with the trips. I miss you terribly. I haven't started showing yet but can begin to feel a tiny moving bulge in my tummy, and it's all your fault, kiddo! So happy that we are going to have a baby and hope and pray the baby, whatever the sex, is healthy and looks like you! Yes, I hope it's a boy; that's always been my wish. From the pictures I've seen of your beautiful daughter, Susan Michelle, you make really beautiful (and handsome, I hope) babies.

Loving you,

Jill

My group of charters to Germany was just completed, and I took several days off to stay in Munich, to rest and recover from the two months of twenty-four-hour entertaining and constant chatter. I was looking forward to sleeping in and just being quiet for a few days. I breakfasted at Pan American's Intercontinental Hotel and was enjoying the peace and quiet when a tap on my shoulder made me turn around. It was the beautiful redheaded senior stewardess from Pacific Southwest Airlines whose card I had discarded several months ago, thinking it was highly unlikely I'd ever see her again. She looked stunning in a bright-red suit and beige blouse. She smiled widely, held out her hand, and reintroduced herself to me.

"Hi!" she exclaimed. "I told you we'd meet again!"

I invited her to join me for breakfast. She reminded me that her name was Melina. She was tall, gorgeous, redheaded, full of vitality…and young! She had remembered my name, Jim Gilchrist, instantly. I ordered black coffee for both of us. Her smile was contagious, and her sense of humor was extraordinary. I was starting to be suspicious of her finding me while I was on furlough and asked her how she came to be in Munich at exactly the same time as my furlough. Melina laughed and said it had taken some fine detective work through some of her fellow airline folks. Now I laughed uncomfortably, but she was so beautiful, I was really happy that she had done the homework to find me.

I started some small talk, trying to cover my initial quick reaction of anger that she had so purposely tracked me down. We chatted and laughed and told airline war stories for over an hour. Melina boldly reached across the table, took my hand in hers, and invited me to her room. Feeling wonderfully twenty again myself, I paid the check quickly, and we almost raced for the room…She demurely let me win, of course! She opened the door quickly, and we rushed to the bed and began undressing each other. Her undergarments were elegant and tasteful—a beige lace bra and matching panties with a half-slip, also beige and silky. She pulled off my shirt and pants and took my jockeys off easily. I had a massive erection as we reclined back into the bed. She laid back in the bed seductively and spread her legs widely. The invitation was irresistible, and I went down on her greedily. She was wet and silky and tasted of love and passion. Her moans turned into screams, and she had several orgasms while I was licking her and kissing the surrounding tender areas.

Still maintaining a massive erection, I inserted myself into her and pushed myself hard inside her. I made sure she had several more orgasms before I finished and filled her with the warm liquid of my own orgasm. We rolled over and kissed for a while and then chatted about our chance meeting. It did not feel very chance to me. I was surprised when Melina said that she had spent months thinking about me and wondering where I was and if she would ever see me again. She smiled and laughed, but she distinctly remembered that I had not offered her *my* card when she'd given me hers on the flight from Seattle to San Fran when we'd first met.

I chatted about the details of my life and brought her up to date on my recent divorce, which had been final now for a couple of months. She asked if "the special girl in San Francisco" was still in my life, and I admitted to a casual affair with an unnamed Jill. Melina wanted to know every detail of my relationship with "the girl in San Francisco" because she remembered that I had called her 'special.' I was reluctant to tell her the whole story of unnamed Jill and especially how current the situation was.

Melina was far more than just stunningly beautiful. She had graduated from Oxford University at seventeen and from Yale summa cum laude, with double Masters degrees in international business and macro economics. I asked her how her multifaceted and complex brain allowed her to be a stewardess, breaking her ass serving drinks to drunks and horny salesmen. She laughed and said she liked the travel and the chances to meet men who were take-charge types and men who were straight at the same time. Even back then San Francisco and Europe were meccas for gays.

We decided to take a shower together, dress, and go for a long walk around Munich. It was Oktoberfest, and the streets of Munich were filled with gaiety overflowing from all shapes and sizes of beer-soaked Germans and boisterous fellow revelers from all nations. Melina and I walked briskly and crossed the street to a tiny café for hot chocolate and more personal conversation. Melina seemed to be asking all the questions, and her unrelenting curiosity about every tiny detail of my life seemed both insatiable and still a little suspicious. We traded the details of our stories and experiences. We laughed mostly at our past mistakes and misjudgments concerning friends and lovers alike. I was as captivated by her intellect as I was by her beauty and came to appreciate her quick mind almost as much as her shapely irresistible body. She seemed to feel the same way. Not only had we become intimate lovers in a short time, but we also shared a common zest for life and for humor, laughter, travel, and adventure. We told dirty jokes and laughed until the little café turned off its lights on us, which was way past the wee hours of the morning.

Melina and I returned to the Intercontinental Hotel, showered, and made insatiable love the rest of the night, right up until dawn. We took an early breakfast knowing our flights would separate us. Mine was back to San Francisco on Pan Am via Frankfurt, and hers was on Lufthansa back to I-didn't-even-ask-where. We agreed loosely to seeing each other in the future and maybe trying to rendezvous for another short jaunt to Europe. No promises were made about "love letters" or messages. Neither of us wanted to interfere with the other's life, and we agreed that long-distance sentimentality was just too inconvenient and would take too much effort and time.

7

[JIM HUMMING: "HOW CAN YOU MEND

A BROKEN HEART?" BY THE BEE GEES]

I RETURNED TO SAN Francisco early in the morning and went straight to my office just off Market Square. I worked for several hours on detailed proposals for upcoming charters and travel packages. I called Jill at her office midmorning and told her I was back and hungry for breakfast. She was thrilled to know that I was home safely and scolded me with her familiar giggle for not answering her telex. I told her that I had rested most of the time but enjoyed hearing from her.

We arranged to have a long breakfast at the Sheraton, and she met me with a wide smile, a warm hug, and a much too lingering kiss on the lips for a public place. I loved it! We were seated at my usual table, 23A, in the Sheraton's grand dining room for the best breakfast in the city. We caught up on our mutual business news and then talked excitedly about our careers. Jill was so thankful to find out that her new firm had not only a very liberal maternity policy but also a very warm and welcoming policy on family obligations and children. She never mentioned whether she had told her new company that she was married or single, and I didn't ask. It was so good to be back *home* in Walnut Creek and to return to some sense of normality. I had missed Jill. She was home to me now, and she had obviously missed me too.

Toward the end of our meal at the Sheraton, Jill asked for the detailed story of Susan Michelle, my daughter, which I had long promised to tell her. Jill was hoping that by now I could discuss Susan Michelle without the pain of the adoption being so raw. I would never be able to discuss Susan Michelle without the pain of the adoption being so raw, but I actually welcomed the opportunity to delve into and relive the greatest memories of my life. I indicated to Herman, my favorite waiter, that we would probably be there quite a while discussing business. He winked and said to take our time. He kept the fresh coffee coming.

"Susan Michelle was the most beautiful baby you could imagine," I told Jill, sounding like the proudest dad in the world, but I fully supported the statement by also telling her that wherever I went with Susan Michelle, people would stop to talk to her and to ogle at her bright smile and her contagious gaiety, but they would compliment *me*, of course, on having such a beautiful daughter! Susan Michelle had been born in Hawaii while I was stationed on a Navy ship in the harbor. She was born at Tripler Army Hospital, which we all called the "pink palace on the hill."

The first time I saw Susan Michelle, I was so excited to see her all healthy, pink, and cuddly. I couldn't take my eyes off her, nor stand to let her out of my sight. I took her everywhere— to picnics at the Pali Pass Lookout on Oahu, to the Punchbowl National Cemetery's beautiful grounds and walking trails, and to the North Shore beaches covered with palm trees. I did not know it was possible to love someone so incredibly much.

Jill interrupted my story to ask if I carried any pictures of Susan Michelle with me. The pictures I had with me were worn and wrinkled. I had carried them with me the entire time while serving with the 4th Marines during the war in Vietnam. The pictures gave me something to fight for and to live for every second of every day. Susan Michelle was fair skinned, with sparkling-blue eyes and wonderfully blond hair with bangs. I had played with her every morning before going on duty at the Long Beach Naval Hospital, where I was stationed during 1967 and 1968. She would awaken as soon as I got up and instantly give me a beguiling smile as she peered at me between her crib's bars. I picked her up, held her, and blew on her tummy until she exploded with giggles. She was a delightfully spirited little girl with golden hair and the brightest smile that captured every person's attention who caught sight of her! Her easy temperament was so warm and inviting, the nurses at Long Beach Naval Hospital were all begging to babysit. Susan Michelle was by far the most precious thing ever to have happened to me and is the greatest love of my life then, now, and forever.

Jill was in tears herself now, mourning with me the loss of my daughter through adoption. To this day I don't know how I found the strength to let Susan Michelle go even with the renowned shrink, Dr. Stein, telling me firmly and repeatedly that it was the best thing I could do for Susan Michelle. Jill, still in tears, patted my hand. Anyway it was and is the hardest decision I've ever had to make.

Years later I would learn that Jill had medical contacts in the Atlanta area and had checked up on Susan Michelle regularly, on my behalf, for years. Jill simply wanted to be able to let me know if Susan ever needed anything or was being mistreated or abused. I prayed hard for Susan Michelle daily, and thank God the bad things never happened to her.

Jill and I ended our breakfast about two in the afternoon. Herman had been a gracious waiter the entire time, even delivering complementary taste treats from the chef to our table between the fresh, hot coffee refills. Jill returned to her office and had to stay there till almost midnight to catch up. She finally drove into our driveway in Walnut Creek a little after midnight, and we sat by the fireplace and talked until almost dawn. She looked radiant and happier than I had ever seen her; I could barely tell she was pregnant, but she didn't join me in any of my multiple rounds of wine and spirits.

We set no alarms and woke to a beautiful free weekend. We ventured down to the Hearst Castle to see the newspaperman's vast empire from the 1920s and '30s. We took Jill's new Caddie convertible and a picnic lunch she prepared for us with homemade pimento-cheese sandwiches on rye, potato salad, slaw, and lots of freshly perked coffee for me in a thermos. I still liked my GTO 389 the best. Being pregnant, Jill said she didn't know which she missed most, wine or coffee.

We stayed overnight at San Simeon's, drove back late Sunday afternoon, and took a quick nap before a light dinner that evening. The weekend passed quickly, as they always did when Jill and I spent time together. Monday arrived too soon, and we both had important business to take care of at our offices, especially Jill, who was hoping to get ahead with all her projects before the baby came. She was taking off eight weeks for maternity leave and had already selected a nanny from the agency her company had recommended, and they were paying for it. I was happy because Jill said the nanny had impeccable credentials, but then I became a little skeptical when I found out her name was ... Mrs. Hitler.

8

[JIM HUMMING: "YOU SHOULD BE DANCING" BY THE BEE GEES

I GOT AN URGENT phone call Sunday night. I discovered that one of my fellow charter reps in New York City had taken ill, and I was assigned to take over the luxury charter. The ten-day trip was from New York to London and Amsterdam. The clients choose the Boeing 747s in first-class configuration, accommodating over 250 execs. They had deluxe accommodations at every juncture of the trip. The execs were GE's best and brightest sales executives, who were being rewarded for having a record sales year in almost every subsidiary.

The flight was to depart on the coming Wednesday and return from Amsterdam ten days later. I told Jill that this evening we'd have to make up on our lovemaking because of ten days' separation and have a special dinner together. She said she'd pick up my suits and other necessities on the way home. She said she wanted to be more intimate than we could be in a restaurant and wanted to fix me something special for dinner at home: broiled fresh Alaskan salmon, salad, and steamed fresh spinach with Verdicchio, our favorite white wine. I arrived home a little after seven and found dinner, music, and candlelight awaiting me.

Jill happily drank fruit juice and milk with her dinner. We did not even linger over our special dinner on Jill's English bone china in front of the fireplace. After dinner I was a little tipsy after having wine and Frangelico for dessert while Jill had homemade custard. We were single-minded and slipped away to bed quickly, leaving the dishes for Mrs. Hitler, who Jill had hired early to be her housekeeper until the baby arrived.

Jill expressed an unusual amount of romantic ardor as we embraced and undressed each other anxiously. We had made love for well over an hour when she wanted us to experiment with a sexual fantasy. She asked me to insert myself into her and stay there overnight while we slept. I was more than willing to follow her desires. We slept till around five, and I awoke gleefully to find myself still inside of her with a large erection. Jill was a wild woman when she awakened, and we made love like crazy for another hour before showering and leaving for the airport. Jill drove me to the San Francisco airport in her Caddie, to the early bird on American Airlines first class to New York City, which departed a little after eight.

I arrived in New York City midafternoon. I spent the entire next day meeting and greeting the key execs of GE, including the CEO, John Sims, and reviewing our itinerary and the services Pan American was providing. Mr. Sims invited me to have lunch in his private dining room and directed some very pointed questions to me about touchy issues that might arise during our schedule. I was excited about this golden opportunity to be of extra personal service to Mr. Sims and the commission I would receive, which was about $5000. The entire price tag was well over $300,000 for the package, which did not even cover the cash tips and other incidentals paid out.

Mr. Sims then introduced me to the additional "special services" I was to be paid handsomely for. He indicated jokingly to me that some of his best people were borderline alcoholics, and some of them loved "the ladies." He asked if I could handle any problems that might arise without his involvement. I assured him we were well trained under these circumstances and had the full support of the sales departments in London and Amsterdam, who maintained extensive contacts in both cities. I also advised him that we had a large cash deposit on standby for any "unusual circumstances"; and that I had direct access to the funds. Of course should we have to use any of these funds, GE would be responsible for reimbursements. Mr. Sims said he had already anticipated that and was prepared to back me up should we have singular or multiple unwelcomed incidents.

The charters were men only; the wives were not happy with those arrangements, but the execs blamed the CEO for that decision, and John Sims knew that too well. I reassured him that my service to his team was twenty-four hours a day, with the support of the local Pan American offices and a large network of land-arrangement subcontractors. At that time Pan American had the largest private telecom network in the world and decades of handling the kinds of concerns John Sims had. Scandals for his company and his reputation were on the line.

I was to spend the next ten days overseeing one hundred and sixty super extroverts, men of the world, and all the *appetites* they had. That meant wine, women, and gambling through the wee hours of the morning. The stakes were high for both of our companies. I felt confident I could handle any circumstances that arose, since I had spent years with Navy and Marine fellas who had the same appetites these men had, but albeit without their budget or good taste in women.

We took off Wednesday morning from New York City, with the Pan American 747 roaring and strutting its stuff down the runway and off into the wild blue wonder toward London. These men had already been partying for days before we took off, and the stews were busy fixing drinks and providing hot finger foods as we leveled off and headed east. Several meals would be served—a lunch after two hours out and a breakfast two hours before our arrival in London. The meals were excellent, with choices of three entrees, sides, and the best wines and liquor. The meals were served on linen tablecloths, and Pan Am even used their best crystal and silverware on these luxury charters.

The Jumbo 747 was a pleasure ark for these fellas and their vices—mostly heavy drinking and flirting with the Pan Am stews. There was one gigantic party throughout the plane. The upstairs lounge was the most popular place to see and be seen. Mr. John Sims held court up there; all the key execs and the sales execs came and went as we cruised at thirty-five thousand feet at over five hundred miles per hour. Being asked up to the sky lounge to see Mr. Sims was an honor all the GE personnel sought, especially if they were anxious for future promotions and upward mobility. The flight cabins rocked with good humor, laughter, and anticipation of arriving in London and proceeding directly to the posh private gambling clubs our tour operators had arranged. Very few of the travelers opted for sleep and rest at the Hotel Dorchester.

Several of my Pam Am counterparts accompanied me to the club Diamond King for the gamblers to unload their booty. Several of the clients won large amounts of loot, around three thousand pounds sterling or approximately $5,600. Most of the others lost hundreds of pounds but enjoyed the well-endowed cocktail waitresses and the opportunities to make female contacts away from home. Thankfully there were no notable troubles. One of our guests drank too much, and my Pan American associates whisked him away, returned him to the hotel, and took him to his room without incident. None of the other guests even noticed the clever withdrawal of one of their own over-indulgers, thanks to my very discreet Pan Am brothers.

Around noon the gambling party returned to the Hotel Dorchester for sleep and a light brunch before the evening partying. I reported to John Sims in his suite about the incident and the activities of his staff and noted there were no scandalous problems. He was pleased and congratulated me on a successful trip over and on my handling of the first day's events. I retired to my suite and took a nice long nap myself before rejoining the partying. I had requested the desk clerk to awaken me at seven for the dinner party planned in the grand ballroom of the hotel. The GE CEO commanded all travelers to be there. The dinner was magnificent, and the drinking continued before and after the dinner. John Sims made a brief statement thanking our Pan Am personnel for such a perfect trip over and for the deluxe accommodations and the luxurious gambling establishment, which he had visited himself only briefly for appearances. I was delighted to hear the loud round of applause from the travelers for our Pan Am staff, including the flight captains, the stew staffs, and the support staffs from Pan Am London. Our clients were all having a great trip!

Over the next four days, we had arranged something for all the travelers, including the aforementioned gambling, a shopping stop so the men could purchase things to take home to their wives and lovers, and three first-class tours through London, Bath, and the Cotswolds. The tours were well balanced, and every traveler had an opportunity to indulge his vices as well as to innocently shop and sightsee.

On day three, while resting in my room, I received a call from our agent at the London Pan Am offices. One of the revelers had had a nasty incident with a top-end call girl at the hotel. The incident involved the hotel detective, the manager of the hotel, and me representing Pan Am. It seemed that one of our more ardent revelers instigated an argument with the madam about the madam's price for a particular young woman, and he had become violent, taking his anger out on the call girl. Our staff notified the hotel, and the detective was allowed into his room to defuse the issue. The traveler was quite drunk and still somewhat violent.

I entered the room along with another Pan Am staffer and the detective. The manager arrived shortly. We calmed down both the call girl and the guest. I paid the amount of the difference between the madam's and the client's understanding of the price of her service. GE would reimburse these funds, as agreed on per my gentlemen's agreement with John Sims. The young man's name was not mentioned in my report to Mr. Sims per his instructions to me.

It was now time to depart for Amsterdam. The big Pan Am jumbo jet arrived on schedule at Heathrow Airport in London and took off immediately for Holland's party city. We arranged a guided tour of the top beer producer in Holland, Heineken, upon our arrival. Of course the "window shopping" for girls of the evening was the favorite destination for many of our guests.

We toured the Heineken beer brewery till late morning and were given unlimited amounts of their fine beer and cheese selections from around Holland. By noon the "herd" was ready for more gambling and more searching for their "young ladies of the evening" and the day, in the case of the "red light district." Thankfully there were no major incidents on our transfer from London to Amsterdam; however, one of the revelers groped one of our more attractive stewardesses, and naturally she handled the situation with professional grace and aplomb. Mr. Sims observed this particular incident and personally chatted with the aggressor and apologized to the young lady. The stewardesses were used to this type of behavior; they were experienced and professionally trained to handle the awkward situations.

The next four days were much like the routine we'd had in London: gambling, drinking, chasing women, tours, and eating junkets around Holland. On our last day, we hosted an early morning outdoor cocktail party at four o'clock. It was a going-home party before we headed back to New York. The revelers had been up all night in private parties; we simply continued the party.

A large tent that would hold over three hundred guests was erected in the middle of a huge tulip farm just outside Amsterdam. The air was cold, around forty-five degrees Fahrenheit, but the giant heaters kept everyone warm even though we could see our exhaled breaths. We continued drinking the finest champagnes and enjoying an open bar filled with a complete selection of top-notch liquors. Many of the men brought their female *guests* and enjoyed the open hot buffet of eggs Benedict, quiche, omelet stations, fresh steamed eel, roasted pork tenderloin, filet mignon, and a huge display of fruits from around the world. Everyone was mostly drunk but in control of their senses and enjoyed the hell out of this "happening" celebration ending the ten days every man would dream about for a lifetime. We celebrated in comfort and style in the middle of over one thousand acres of tulips of every color as the sun rose to greet us.

The jumbo jet was awaiting our arrival at Schiphol airport with engines screaming to warm up for the eight-hour trip back to New York City. We boarded her around noon, and the drinking and partying continued for the younger salesmen. The older guys caught up on sleep and mixed with the beautiful stewardesses hand selected for this particular charter. The flight was pleasant, and as we approached New York City I was looking forward to three to four days off to rest and recoup from ten days of twenty-four-hour duty. One of the stews recognized me from an earlier charter to Amsterdam. We chatted for some time before she invited me to spend the night with her in Manhattan. I was very tired but accepted her generous offer, and we took a cab from JFK to her expensive apartment in the middle of Manhattan off Park Avenue.

"Wow!" I said. "You can afford a place like this on a stew's salary?!"

She smiled and said that her "sugar daddy" covered all of her living expenses, and that she saved most of her own money. I was concerned about "daddy" showing up unexpectedly, but she assured me he was in Japan for a month, and she had talked to him at the airport to make sure he was where he was supposed to be. Her name was Gail. We were almost too tired to sleep, and I was tired of drinking. I fixed her a late-night martini—a double to be exact. We decided to relax in her large garden tub. We soaked and talked for almost an hour and a half. Too tired for sex? Yes, both of us! We decided to sleep into the next day and then reconsider our sexual needs.

I awoke around noon to find Gail giving me a super blowjob. She was wearing red-lace panties, a red-lace bra, and a New York Yankees baseball hat with her blond ponytail swinging out the back. She pulled her panties off and mounted me like the Royal Canadian Police; we banged each other all the early afternoon. After hours of great sex, we were famished. We showered, dressed, and headed for the Manhattan Ritz. The restaurant served breakfast all day, and we ordered a mountain of omelets, champagne, and quiche.

It was refreshing to be away from the revelers and the excesses they enjoyed. Gail was amazing in bed, and in her favor she also had a quick wit, a good sense of humor, and surprising intelligence. She had grown up in Seattle and graduated from Cal State in Los Angeles. We teased and joked and spent the afternoon seeing the parks and sights around New York City. At 7:00 p.m., we retreated back to the "sugar daddy's" place. I spent several days with Gail before flying back to San Francisco on American. I always traveled first class as a fellow airline employee and enjoyed a nice long nap before arriving in San Francisco. I had telexed Jill upon my arrival in New York City and indicated that I'd be home in a couple of days. She met me at baggage claim and had her big red Caddie parked in the no-parking zone as usual. We hugged and kissed and rushed to the Caddie before having to deal with the unfriendly cop standing just outside.

It was comforting to be *home*. We had amazingly loving sex during the early evening, showered, and slept soundly wrapped in each other's arms. Jill let me feel her stomach move with the baby's kicks, and instantly I missed Susan Michelle deeply but did not let Jill know. Jill and I happily settled back into a routine, and I returned to my Pan Am office in San Francisco the next morning.

9

THE COMING MONTHS were pretty routine—more charters and sales calls in between helping Jill with her pregnancy. I was fortunate to be in San Francisco when the baby arrived. It was a boy, as Jill had wished. When he was born, I took several days off to settle our new little one into her house in Walnut Creek. Jill named the child David James Meadows, as we had agreed, giving him her last name and including me with the middle name. She maintained her position of wanting no strings attached to me in regards to his upkeep and nurturing. Jill seemed at peace with our arrangement, and the housekeeper, Mrs. Hitler, turned out to be the child-care giver her accolades had proclaimed her to be. David was a beautiful child, and yes, he looked just like me, as Jill had wanted. Even with the child and her superlative attentiveness as a mother, Jill continued to flourish in her career.

In mid-1971, Pan American hosted a huge conference and invited all of our key contractors to London for a one week. It was a first-class affair and gave all the charter reps an opportunity to meet the owners, the higher management folks, and the wholesalers who arranged all of our hotels, cars, tours, meals, and entertainment and anything we required to close our deals with the Fortune 500 firms. The conference was held in the Hotel Dorchester's grand ballroom, where both Pan Am management and the tour operator owners conferred on mutual matters concerning our services and the expenses needed to operate. Both parties had opportunities to exchange ideas and provided seminars on specific issues such as cost and limits of liability to our mutual clients.

Pan Am paid for all the facilities for the week, but the wholesaler owners wined and dined us, particularly the ones who worked with us on a one-on-one basis. We mutually profited by bringing business to these companies in their winter off-season months, which provided capital for both Pan Am and the tour operators. This mutually beneficial arrangement kept Pan Am jets flying and payrolls up to date. The tour operators where able to fill up hotels and book great deals on the packages we selected to go along with our charter aircraft sales.

Returning to my room around eight after a lavish dinner, I received a hand-delivered note addressed to Mr. Jim Gilchrist from a tour operator I had used many times. The note asked if I would please join a Mr. Leo Halaby of Inter-World for an early breakfast in his suite. I confirmed to the messenger that I would be honored to meet the owner of Inter-World and join him for breakfast at 6:00 a.m. sharp. I did not realize that this meeting would change my life forever beyond anything I could have imagined. His company was considered to be the very best travel consortium by most of the airlines, both international and domestic carriers. I had some difficulty going to sleep now wondering why a global entrepreneur of Mr. Halaby's caliber would request my presence at a private breakfast with him. What could he possibly want with a mere luxury-charter-rep salesman?

At 5:00 a.m. my wake-up call came, and I showered and dressed for the day. The uniform of the day was casual pants and shirts; even the top execs from both companies dressed in a very casual manner. I arrived at Mr. Halaby's room on time, and he personally welcomed me at the door. He greeted me with a firm handshake and invited me into his spacious suite of rooms, which smelled of hot breakfast and coffee; I also noted he had a very nice champagne on ice. I was curious about champagne this early in the morning. Mr. Halaby just laughed at my curiosity about a celebratory drink so early.

Leo Halaby appeared to be in his seventies; he was tall and slender and of Middle Eastern decent, probably Iranian or Syrian. He had a broad, all-encompassing smile and seemed totally content with life. He was filled with confidence and genuinely was interested in my comfort and well-being. His assistant, a tall, dark woman with green eyes, also of Middle Eastern decent; offered me coffee and led me to the table where we were served a sumptuous almost American breakfast of scrambled eggs, sausages, and croissants. The coffee was very strong, but I became used to it after several cups.

Mr. Halaby insisted that I call him Leo, and I offered the same response, asking him to call me Jim. His assistant was very beautiful, and I detected some flirting with her eyes before she left us alone to talk in private. Leo congratulated me on a record year of charters and the business I had sent his way. He stated that he was impressed with and had seen my sales records with Pan American Airways and that I had sold over $3 million in luxury charters and over $2 million dollars in land arrangements with his firm alone. He thanked me for the record year he had also enjoyed due to my efforts.

Leo wanted to know if Inter-World took good care of me during my two months off during March and April.

"Yes!" I exclaimed. The hotels, cars, meals, and private tours around southern France and the Amalfi coast were particularly pleasant. My expenses were also generously taken care of by Inter-World in London, Amsterdam, and Germany. The gratuitous services his company had provided for me were extraordinary.

Leo continued, "Did you enjoy the company of my young ladies who acted as our sales staff and tour guides? I just refer to them as my 'granddaughters.' I take such good care of them too that they all want to be family."

I laughed and said they were charming in *every way* possible. He again laughed out loud and smiled with a devilish grin as we both laughed.

"And did my staff provide you with special thank-you notes along the way during your vacations?"

Again I said the cash was very generous but not needed after he had picked up all of my other expenses in March and April. He assured me that there could be even more profitable years to come in my future. That sounded great!

Leo indicated to me that he had already asked my Pan Am boss to allow me to accompany him back to Cyprus. I was taken aback at this invitation and his assumption that I would go. He had been born in Iran but had moved to Cyprus when he was a child. Over the years he had learned more than twelve languages, including Chinese, Russian, and Dutch. His business acumen was incredible, and his reputation at the airlines was legendary. I guessed that he was in his seventies, but he was in great physical shape and appeared to work out, walk, or exercise on a regular basis. His good health, he said, was passed down from his father and grandfather. He had observed that I too was in good shape, and he knew that I had served as a Navy Corpsman with the Marines during the Vietnam War. Leo also knew the details of my service record and congratulated me on my decorations received during the Vietnamese War in 1968 and 1969.

I was a little suspicious that he seemed to have *checked me out* so thoroughly, but I thanked him for his kind, all-knowing comments and compliments, and we lingered over our breakfast and the hot coffee that just kept coming. I was still curious about the very expensive Taittinger champagne on the table next to us. Leo smiled and said he might want to share that with me at the conclusion of our breakfast. I asked him what the occasion was, and he reminded me of the multimillion-dollar record sales year that *we* had just completed. Leo said that he had made an incredible profit while his competitors had just struggled through the past winter season. He asked if I would be willing to accompany him back to Cyprus.

"Of course," I said. "I would be honored." That seemed to be the answer he had hoped for and the reason for celebration. Now he broke open the champagne.

10

[JIM HUMMING: "MONEY, THAT'S WHAT
I WANT" BY BARRETT STRONG]

LEO HALABY AND I left for Cyprus early Saturday morning on
his own private Gulfstream jet. Aboard he had several lovely
ladies serving us a light breakfast of grapefruit and poached eggs
along with the best fresh-ground coffee I had ever tasted. Leo indicated that it would take us only several hours to reach his private
airfield. I had never traveled to Cyprus before but heard from my
fellow charter reps that it was beautiful and enchanting, and the
women there were gorgeous and very *active*. They loved to dance
and drink good wine.

During our trip Leo broke out a bottle of Dom Perignon, and
we enjoyed his fine champagne right up to landing time. We had
a smooth flight and even smoother landing. I found out that the
pilot was a retired Pan American captain who was now living in
Cyprus as Leo's personal pilot. I was thrilled with the junket and
the leisure time to be away from the busy office for several days.

I telexed Jill about my side trip to Cyprus and told her I should be home in about four days. She replied that she missed me and that David was a wonderful child, sleeping, playing, and eating when he was awake. It was comforting to hear from "home base" and from someone I knew loved me without reservations whatever I did or wherever I went. To say Jill was classy is a gross understatement.

Leo's staff took my bags to a secluded room overlooking a magnificent garden with a beautiful fountain. One of his shapely staff members unpacked my bags and put my things away. Leo joked that all the young women at his house were his want-to-be "granddaughters" and that I should be respectful to them at all times.

I took a nap, showered for our evening meal, and joined Leo and several of his "granddaughters" for a sumptuous meal. We laughed and joked about the business and the differences in the Western philosophies versus the Middle Eastern way of life.

Leo stated, "Westerners are far too serious about their work habits and do not relax and enjoy the pleasures of life nearly enough."

After dinner Leo gave me a tour of his immense compound, which was old-world stunningly beautiful. The breathtaking landscaping alone must have cost millions, and the old-world Italian villa was a work of art in every respect. He instructed me to make myself at home and ask for anything I needed from his "granddaughters," who would be pleased to attend to my every need, and he meant everything. He asked me to meet him for lunch the next day in his immense study, which had a magnificent fireplace and *objets d'art* from around the world.

Late in the evening, I retired to my bedroom, which had a small fire already glowing in the fireplace; it was chilly from the ocean breezes. I washed my face and prepared for bed. When I returned to my bed, there was a beautiful young woman in a sheer nightgown with a big smile on her face. She asked if she was acceptable as my bed partner for the evening. I nodded a grand approval and slid into bed next to her. She pulled my jockeys down, put me into her mouth, and caressed the rest of me with gentle hands, and I was lost in her green eyes and olive complexion. I discovered the next morning she was from a small region in Iran where tall, blond, and blue or green-eyed women of Aryan descent were common. I had heard from my Pan Am counterparts that these women were considered to be the most beautiful women in the world.

The next morning we had coffee and continued our lovemaking. Her name was Naomi, and not only was she beautiful and clever but also she had a great sense of humor and fitted into the top-ten lays I had ever had. She laughed that we seemed to have learned some *new tricks* in our bed the night before. I certainly did. On her way out, she gently reminded me of my appointment with Leo at noon.

Another "granddaughter" welcomed me into Leo's study, and I settled into a very comfortable couch next to the fireplace. The cool air continued for the next few days, coming in from the Mediterranean Sea. A beautiful staff served us breakfast, and then Leo dismissed them all. I noticed a lingering older, dark-skinned Indian who did not leave. I had glimpsed him before in the shadows around Leo. The older Indian gentleman was dressed all in white and sat silently and humbly on the floor about ten feet away from Leo. He was much too lithe for me to assume he was a bodyguard.

Leo settled in next to me and revealed a file he had created about me and my background. The file was thick; an expert had vetted me. Leo smiled and commented that he and I had had many of the same experiences: combat fighting in a war, the love of fine women, good food, wine, music, and keen business acumen. Leo was particularly impressed with my exceptional luxury-charter sales record with Pan Am, which I had accrued in such a short time, and the broad network of international contacts I had amassed both inside and outside of my Pan American business. Leo stated that his associate staff members throughout Europe and the Middle East preferred to do business with me and had enjoyed their off hours with me at the finest restaurants, bars, and cabarets I had selected. I was flattered hearing the accolades from such a worldly, enlightened man but also felt very vulnerable to have been watched through Leo's fine microscope, which spanned my entire life.

Leo turned serious quickly in both his tone and his body language. He asked me bluntly what I had planned for the rest of my life, noting that I was twenty-five. He knew about Jill and also named the other women I had had relationships with. I was taken aback and felt more than a little uncomfortable sitting in the presence of someone who seemed to know as much about my life as I did.

Leo had asked about my future plans. The subject had come up many times among my Pan Am buddies, and we often speculated what the future held for our lives. For the most part, we felt so young that wealth and fame were distant dreams in the future for all of us. Many of my contemporaries were already married with several children, were single and playing the field, or were recently engaged. I was the confirmed bachelor of the group. They did not know about Jill and only knew that I lived in Walnut Creek, which was far enough away from them that they did not know my private business or situation.

Leo had put the question to me about my future goals, and I was on the spot to respond. I felt restless, somewhat defensive, and totally unprepared to give a serious answer. I was content with my life but did feel a yearning to be more financially independent during the turbulent 1970s.

He smiled and said, "There's a much bigger life out there that is perfectly suited to you and your global savvy that you haven't even considered yet, my friend."

I asked him to explain.

"There is no more fruitful life than to be independent in finance, family, and friends—free from governmental intrusion into your life and free from taxes that drain the lifeblood and ambition out of you. I would like to offer you an opportunity to attain all that," Leo continued. He delivered to me a new vision of the enriched life within my reach. I asked him to continue. Leo talked philosophy and business with me for over two hours, laying out for me plans to achieve financial goals I had never dreamed of. To be completely financially independent, to escape government intrusion and high taxes without looking over my shoulder as I traveled, and to *wheel and deal* with Inter-World's international contacts all sounded too good to be true. Leo held his looking glass into my soul. He confessed that he had no sons and was convinced that I was the right person to groom into his way of life, and he had certainly done his homework. The bottom line was power—enough power to be free from all the negative financial aspects of life. I was twenty-five years old, and Leo had awakened in me the idea of an unimaginably lucrative future.

Leo then laid out his specific plans for my life. I would continue to work with Pan American as usual. Leo cleverly made a vague reference to the advantages I had being free from customs and from being searched for contraband. My pristine reputation with Pan American had allowed me the privilege of never being challenged or searched for drugs or any other illegal items. I had made sure over the past years to make close friends with the customs boys, gifting them with top-notch booze or fixing them up with my castaway girlfriends. The customs agents knew I was spotlessly clean when it came to bringing in illegal drugs or contraband. Leo Halaby had done his research well. He knew this information about me in detail and had gone to great lengths to check this out in both the United States and the countries I flew into with Pan Am. He also knew that I had a detailed overview of the customs agents and the one-way mirrors they used to observe both travelers and airline folks alike. Leo already had his proof that I knew all the folks on both sides of the mirrors.

I asked Leo what the bottom line would be for me. He laughed out loud and said, "Imagine having millions of dollars, pounds, rubles, francs, rupees, yen, and all the known currencies around the world. Your funds would be free from all taxes and records that government agencies could track. You can keep your current arrangements with your ladies as long as they continue to know you only as a simple luxury-charter rep for one of the most renowned airlines on Earth." He continued with an even longer list of opportunities that I would have under these circumstances. I asked him how?

Leo asked me to consider being a "special courier" for his diamonds and fine stones around the world, mostly in Europe and the Middle East and occasionally in Asia. My hands broke out in a sweat. I had a chill running up my spine, and Leo astutely read my concerns from the look on my face.

"It's a challenge, Jim," he stated, "a challenge to change from a lack of control over your life to one of power, the life of a savvy and comfortable gentleman of the world."

Leo urged me to consider his proposal. I agreed with the general premise of his plan without thinking too much about it. He had obviously been extremely successful with Inter-World, gauging from his luxurious style of living and the international freedoms he enjoyed around the world. Leo had over three thousand employees in his conglomerate of international businesses; most were in the travel wholesale business, but Leo was the owner of several small airlines, businesses, and banks all over the world. He had the funds, contacts, infrastructure, and balls to carry out his plans uninterrupted by governments and undaunted by crime families. I now saw Leo as my beneficent *Dutch uncle* and was honored that he would consider me as his protégé and would include me as a legacy to his future. Leo wanted to be my benefactor and already had a net worth of $30 billion dollars; mostly in liquid funds and essential services, such as the perpetual need for luxury travel and accommodations, even during a depression.

Leo and I talked for most of the day, with a late lunch brought in while we continued to talk in private. No one disturbed our talks, not even the "granddaughters." I was struck by the stark contrast between my life now and what it would become if I accepted his offer. I was weighing the possibilities as to whether I should risk my career with Pan American and probably some significant international prison time for an unknown opportunity to be truly financially independent from any man or government. It was the opportunity of a lifetime to attain true power.

Leo asked me to consider his offer over the next day. We were both departing Cyprus in two days. We were enjoying Leo's finest Scotch. Before leaving me for the day, Leo said, "I have no male heirs myself and have chosen you very carefully, and you know me by worldwide reputation. You would have at your disposal all of my political and business contacts. All the actual transactions would be processed by true professional handlers of the items being transported through customs stations and the other areas of official jurisdiction, namely the local and international police."

The gamble was a mutual risk for both of us. I was tempted, but I would be putting my youth and future in danger because of the possibilities of impending years in an international prison or the grim prospects of my return to employment in the legitimate world.

Leo and I had a final Scotch and left smiling about our marathon discussion. I went to my room to take a nap—or tried to nap with all that was running through my head. Leo left to oversee his local responsibilities while I wandered the estate after my attempted nap. In all honesty his proposal excited me, and just considering the possibilities gave me a sense of euphoria. We were to meet again the next day for an early breakfast, and Leo expected my answer then after I had had time to consider his offer and sleep on it overnight. Since I was free for dinner, I invited Naomi to join me. We met around seven and drank lots of Leo's good local wine before being served dinner. The dinner included standing rib roast, local fresh vegetables grown on Leo's estate, and a Cypriot *sharlotta* dessert that Naomi had made just for me. We sat by the fire after dinner with coffee and Frangelico and told jokes from our different cultures.

Naomi was curious about why Leo had brought me to his estate. I told her we had business to discuss about the upcoming charter season. Naomi laughed and said it must be pretty important for Leo to bring a younger man all the way out here; she indicated that most of his close associates, the ones who visited Leo at his home, were older men about his age. Naomi thought Leo might be considering an associate for his waning years.

I asked her about how many "granddaughters" Leo had? Again her laughter was spontaneous and loud. "All the women in Leo's life are his granddaughters. He tells us jokingly that he calls us all granddaughters because we are all really nice to him, hoping he'll remember us in his will." She also confided in me that Leo was still a very virile man with a huge sexual appetite, and that dozens of women around the world looked forward to bedding him... and his money. Naomi and I decided to go to bed ourselves around eleven. I drank lots of wine.

"It has been said that too much wine dulls the sexual appetite in most men," she stated teasingly.

I quickly retorted, "Don't you know that's only true for dull men, Miss Naomi?"

She giggled, loved the irony, and loved adding a new line to her repertory of boudoir jokes and funny comebacks. I stopped her giggling at once by taking her down onto the bed, going down on her, and eating her gently till she became extremely wet and very hot. She spread her legs high toward the ceiling and pulled a nearby pillow under her. She was wet and ready for me, and I inserted myself into her and banged her mercilessly. She screamed out loud and moaned over and over for at least an hour as I banged her and slid into every position we could imagine. We fell asleep happily wrapped in each other's arms until my wake-up call at eight.

A light breakfast of fresh local fruits and fresh hot breads was served to me in my room. Naomi showered and then joined me for a croissant before I left to meet Leo at ten for coffee. Leo went straight to the point and wanted my answer right away, since he was leaving late that night for further business dealings. I was scheduled to leave the next morning to New York City then on to San Francisco.

Leo was smiling as I tried to get the affirmative words out without choking or showing my flushed face. "Yes," I said. He broke out in pure pleasant laughter and gave me the hardy gentleman's Italian hug. "When do I start?"

Leo answered, "Today, my son!" He led me downstairs to a large workshop where several craftsmen were working on the instruments that would be used in our *courier* service. Leo showed me an expensive pair of shoes with a false sole in each shoe. Inside the false soles, his assistant poured several million dollars' worth of diamonds of perfect clarity, fire, and color. In addition to the shoes, his workers had produced a series of especially designed briefcases, one of which would be identical to the one I would exchange with the mystery contact at the Pan Am Clipper Club. Leo said I should carry the briefcase the next day on my way back to San Francisco.

He continued, "Upon your arrival at the JFK airport in New York City, you will meet your first associate. He will meet you in the Pan Am Clipper Club. There you will adjourn to the men's room and swap the shoes and the briefcase under the stalls and continue on your journey."

I laughed. "How did you know my shoe size?"

Leo replied that he was always ahead of the curve with what was to come! He impressed on me that my contact would not introduce himself but would be waiting on me in the stalls in the men's room of the Clipper Club.

"How will I know which is the right man?"

Leo said that it was already planned, just to slide my shoes and then the briefcase under the stall where a *Boys' Life* magazine would be on the floor. My briefcase was filled with eight large leather bags of top-quality diamonds.

I reluctantly asked Leo what my take was for this service. He immediately replied that upon safe delivery and transfer of the shoes and briefcase $250,000 would be deposited into the bank account of my choice. Leo's bookkeeper, Walter Kosky, would arrange for the direct deposit into my account and even help me select banks and set up the accounts if needed. Leo casually mentioned that obviously there would be no tax record of the transaction, since he owned the bank there in Cyprus and also the bank in London as well as banks in several other countries throughout Europe and Asia where we did business.

Later that afternoon I met with Walter Kosky, who handled all of Leo's fund transfers. I choose four of Leo's banks and called each bank to set up an account via phone and telex where my funds would be deposited. I chose London, Munich, Amsterdam, and Paris for my accounts with equal amounts to be transferred into each of the four accounts after each venture was completed. Additionally I had arranged an account in Victoria, British Columbia, in Canada, for additional transfers for liquidity if Jill and I needed funds when we visited her cottage in Anacortes. Perhaps in the future I would be able to purchase my own property in Anacortes or Victoria.

11

[JIM HUMMING: "TAKE ME OUT TO THE
BALL GAME" BY RONNIE NEUMAN]

LEO HALABY DEPARTED for Hong Kong late that evening via Haifa, Israel, New Delhi, and Bangkok. Upon Leo's departure he embraced me firmly, and I asked if he had any words of wisdom for my first trip.

He smiled and said, "Drink moderately, smile a lot, say hello to old friends, but avoid long discussions or frowns around the authorities. Relax, enjoy the first-class travel and the arms of your older lover in San Francisco. You'll be a very rich man in a few short years; then you'll be ready for even bigger fish." He added, "I know it'll be hard for you, but avoid strange girly bedfellows on these trips."

We both laughed, but I knew I would avoid acquaintances of any kind because the chance of any snafu at all before the courier exchange was made could cost me millions of dollars at least and hopefully not my life. I did not know yet what Leo's other investors and partners were capable of.

I slept with Naomi once more before I left, which of course involved no sleep at all. We made love like two excited honeymooners in heat. We had also developed a close friendship that was enhanced further because she had learned that I would be a "special agent" for Leo. I was really looking forward to being a financially free man and not the Jill's kept man, a life that I had fallen into. Jill never complained, saying I would always be welcomed wherever she was. I wondered how David was doing and actually missed seeing them both.

Leo's private Gulfstream was waiting on me at his private runway. I departed Cyprus at 7:00 a.m. with my "brand-new shoes," my newly configured briefcase, and a broad smile on my face. I was mentally prepared for this trip but was still smartly anxious about the consequences for failure. Of course Leo's name would never be mentioned if a failure occurred. Leo assured me that if the worst happened, he had the finest lawyers available around the world who were specialists in international law and national law in every major country where we did business.

The jet arrived in London at noon, and I immediately headed for the Pan American Clipper Club with my briefcase. My luggage had been transferred to Pan Am's 747 "over the pole" trip to San Francisco. I had a Maker's Mark and an Amstel beer to relax and reflect on my recent career change. It was so good, I had another round. Then it was time to visit the men's room at the Club. The restrooms were extremely posh and cleaned minute by minute by the Pan American service staff. I walked down the row of stalls and discovered only one stall was occupied. It was exactly 1:00 p.m., and I took the empty stall next to the mystery man. I was seated and looked down at the floor of the stall next to me. Yes! Just as planned, there immediately appeared a *Boys' Life* magazine. I slipped off the multimillion-dollar loafers and slid them over to the next stall along with the briefcase. The exchange of the shoes and the briefcase was quick and smooth. Not one word was spoken, and I exited the stall immediately and went back for another round of my favorite booze and chaser. Having done the deed, my relief was instant, but I was still somewhat apprehensive during the coming hours.

The jumbo Boeing 747 was on time. Arriving safely in San Francisco was another tremendous relief, and yes, Jill was there waiting on me; I had telexed her from the Clipper Club. She had arranged for Mrs. Hitler to take care of David while we drove back to Walnut Creek. Mrs. Hitler was a live-in service housekeeper with glowing nanny credentials, and Jill had even had an extra room added for her off the main house. Jill sensed there was something special about my glowing expression and good humor. We drank for several hours, and I caught her up on all my legitimate Pan American business issues. Jill assumed the good humor was due to the success of my Pan Am luxury charters, and I would not divulge any other reasons.

Jill caught me up on David and how her job was progressing. She had received a large salary increase and said it would be easier now to "take care of me" ...I had to laugh out loud; she could not know how much I had just made on one trip home. We went to bed after several rounds of drinks and a peek at little David. We made gentle, romantic love for several hours and finally both drifted off into a deep, well-deserved sleep.

The next morning I returned to my office and caught up on all the pending business I had for the next winter season. I had already booked twelve luxury charters to begin in September and run till my two-month vacation in March and April. Six of the charters were first-class jumbo-jet packages. I had already telexed Leo's company for the land arrangements to be scheduled. Every week I always followed up with a phone call to Walter Kosky, my funds manager, and Mr. Spiros, my contact with Leo's company. I waited several days to verify that my funds had been deposited into my accounts. I checked in via phone with my rep at each bank; the funds had all been deposited as promised. In fact the funds were deposited the day after my trip.

To date no questions or inquiries had been made of me as I went about my daily routine with Pan American. My boss even came by and asked how I had liked the seminar in London. I smiled, thanked him for asking me, and told him the seminar was very rewarding and that I had learned so much from the trip.

The charters were stacking up well, and I had reached my quota of twenty-five charters by July. I advised Mr. Spiros, my travel contact that Leo had assigned to me, of my scheduled charters and the dates, times, and places I would be going beginning in September. Leo asked my contact to see if I could arrange trips for "our business" over the next few weeks.

I answered, "Yes, I could schedule recon trips to match his needs." I would check out hotels and meet with his contractors on the upcoming charter trips scheduled between September and February. During my spring vacation, I could travel literally anywhere he needed with my Pan Am sales ID and enjoy the travel perks and privileges arranged by our sales office, which asked no questions about where or when I chose to travel. These factors gave great flexibility to both Leo and me. We both had carte blanche on our time and money to be invested in our mutual business.

I essentially closed out my business year in July, with only paperwork, schedule updates, and coordination with Leo's wholesalers from Europe to the Middle East. I had three assistants who took care of client changes in their itineraries, upgrades, and all the details of the charters. My contact for Leo, Mr. Spiros, wanted me to run a "courier service" within the next week. I set up a recon trip with Pan Am for myself to our rendezvous city, London. There I met the honorable Mr. Spiros at our favorite spot, the old St. Ermin's Hotel. We both laughed at how close this location was to one of our nemeses, the New Scotland Yard.

The hotel was a top first-class older hotel with great service staff who had earned their credentials and fine reputation over decades. The services were complete and efficient. On my arrival on a chilly day for July, I sent out a double Glenlivet to the baggage master, Johnny Cain. He raised his glass, smiled, and winked at me, knowing "my usual" included his recommendations of the best girls in the neighborhood. Mr. Spiros and I settled in at the bar while our bags were deposited in our very large, old-fashioned rooms with high ceilings and the most comfortable over-sized chairs and beds. The windows were tall but could still be opened for spring breezes and to observe Johnny Cain work his magic with the unknown services he had provided certain regular clients for over thirty years.

While Mr. Spiros and I were still at the bar, Johnny Cain casually joined us for a round; Johnny advised us to have our hair cut at the hotel barber shop. He winked and advised us that the young ladies there gave great head for a reasonable tip. Additionally, the girls would shine your shoes overnight if you left them outside your door, and one shoe pointing in the opposite direction indicated you were interested in some *nookie* for a very reasonable price, usually about fifty American dollars. They would contact you about your shoes and work out a time for their "services". So, adding in the stewardesses who stayed at the hotel plus the "service gals," we had it made in the shade.

Mr. Spiros and I adjourned to his room, where he provided me with the details of the services Leo wanted done over the next several days. The trip again was scheduled for Rome and New York City. Spiros would provide the other details and the objects needing transport would be provided by Spiros shortly. He discussed in great detail with me the plans and when and where we were to begin. I would act as a courier from London to Rome on Pan American's Clipper and meet with our contact there. That was project one; the second service would be back to London from Rome, again with courier items. Finally the last service was a delivery back to New York City.

I would receive payment for each of the three courier services. I asked Spiros the take on my part. He stated that it should be around $750,000, which Walter Kosky would deposit into my accounts via Leo's London Inter-World bank. I surmised that these courier items must be pretty valuable merchandise. Mr. Spiros shrugged and said it was just business as usual. However, I was to find out that the amount of merchandise would be weighed in size and bulk. He held special luggage in his room for the trips. As we drank and laughed, I thought about meeting Gail again in New York City and her red NY Yankees cap! That would be the icing on the cake for this trip.

Mr. Spiros and I spent two days drinking, eating, and enjoying the ladies, both the pros and novices. On the third day, I left for Rome with my new bags and briefcase. I arrived at Fiumicino or Leonardo da Vinci airport in Rome around noon—lunchtime and naptime for the Italians. Pan American's service staff quickly cleared my luggage with no customs inspections of any kind. I breathed a sigh of relief and smiled.

The plans called for me to meet a woman at the Grand Hotel who would be wearing a gold-colored dress with extra-large pearls and a large, feathered hat. Arriving at the Grand Hotel, I saw her in the bar with a pink champagne and a slight grin on her face. There were no introductions except to say the code words Spiros and I were given by Leo himself. The words were "life is good aboveground." The response was "dirt naps are no fun for us." The contact was confirmed. I gave her my baggage keys, except for my one overnight carry-on bag, and instructed the bellhop to place the bags in her car just outside the side entrance. She smiled, gave me the European peck on each cheek, and drove away, not to be seen again for months. The first leg of our courier service was completed.

I spent the night at the Grand, and several new luggage bags were delivered to my room that night. I did not open the luggage. The bags were somewhat heavy, but there would be no issue with my unlimited weight carriage on Pan Am. I departed Fiumicino airport around noon, arrived in London, and cleared customs cheerfully without ever having my bags weighed or inspected. Again I checked in to the St. Ermin's and waved at Johnny. I sent out a triple to him this time. He was delighted with the new fuel and took the shot in one gulp.

I had my usual room reserved, and Spiros joined me later in the bar, where we had three rounds and flirted with several Lufthansa stewardesses just checking in. We received smiles, and two came over to join us. We partied with Ursula and Christina in the bar until dinner and invited them to join us. They were delighted to share dinner and whatever came after our meals. Christina joined me in my room after dinner, and I ordered champagne and chocolates to celebrate the evening. She asked me to undress her very slowly. I undid her blouse and unbuttoned her skirt, and she slipped out of her shoes. Then I took off her beige panties and then her garter belt and hose. We stood kissing for a long time before she started breathing hard and walked me gently over to the bed. She asked me to lie on my back while she slipped between my legs and worked her magic, which made me bigger and bigger by the second. She removed her beige bra and displayed a magnificent set of tits; her nipples were hard and shaped like cherries. She sucked me for a very long time until she achieved the very wet ending she wanted. She wanted my sweet liquid all over her. I complied willingly, and she was delighted with her conquest. Next she massaged me all over, really all over, and forced me into another good erection; this time I turned her on her side and banged her from behind. She screamed loudly at first and then moaned as I banged her over and over. Not all the stewardesses were this good. We drank more Taittinger champagne and nibbled on the chocolate-covered cherries from the assortment on the silver tray the St. Ermin's staff had sent up complimentary with the champagne, and we managed a short nap before dawn.

The stewardesses had an early morning flight to Munich, so they left our rooms at 5:00 a.m. Spiros and I had breakfast at seven; I was to take the Pan American jumbo jet headed to New York City at ten. We adjourned to his room, and he provided me with the new luggage I was to transport along with my own matching carry-on suit bag. I ordered champagne and put it on Spiros's expense account. He congratulated me on the success so far and wished me luck in New York City.

I had contacted Gail the day before, and she sounded anxious and delighted to see me again at her sugar daddy's place in Manhattan. We had only one day before I was to leave for San Francisco. The jumbo Pan Am jet arrived in New York City on time. Again my bags were cleared without question, and I used the same procedure I had used earlier, except instead of a *Boys' Life* magazine, it was *Mad* magazine this time!

Gail was waiting on me outside the JFK terminal in a yellow cab and ran up to hug and kiss me passionately. We went immediately to the sugar daddy's place, and we both ran for the king-size bed. While we undressed each other, her roommate joined us for a threesome. We all laughed at the same time, anticipating the good sex we expected from each other. I lived up to their expectations and wore them both out with sex until my legs were weak. I watched the girls enjoy each other for a while until I got another erection. Ready to go again, I took them both again until we all collapsed on the bed. We adjourned to the large hot tub and then showered together before heading out for a late dinner. We went out dancing at an upscale private club the girls frequented, and we danced till midnight.

We adjourned back to the sugar daddy's just after midnight. We all had early flights out the next morning, so we collapsed into a needed sleep. We promised to do this again as soon as possible. Gail's girlfriend gave me her card and said she'd like to join me on one of my flights to Europe since she had never flown internationally. Her name was Beth, and she was extraordinarily beautiful, high spirited, and also one of the best partners in bed I had ever had. She was also a champion female lover, but I threw her card away too.

I arrived back in San Francisco via American Airlines, again in first-class accommodations. On the way home, I stopped by the office, spent several hours catching up with my assistants, and brought my business house in order. I called Jill at work, and she squealed with delight that I was home safely. I had telexed her every day of my trip. On the way to Walnut Creek, I stopped by Zack's in Sausalito, had a couple of bloody marys, and asked the waiter to bring me a phone. I called my account rep, Walter

Kosky, who confirmed that all my funds had been deposited into my international accounts. I now had a cool million in my accounts. I paid my bill, including the international calls, and left for Walnut Creek to reunite with Jill and David.

12

JILL AND I had an evening to discuss my trips and look in on little David; he and the nanny, Mrs. Hitler, were fast asleep. We had some drinks by the fire and talked about the future. Jill hinted that her company had approached her about opening an office just outside London. She would be the Interim Director making double her present salary in the San Francisco area, and the job promised to evolve into her being the full-time Director of International Medical Corps of London. I was very excited for her, and we toasted our crystal glasses and hugged tightly. I would never be able to reveal to her my current lucrative arrangements with Leo. There was no need to, and I had promised Leo that our agreements were personal and confidential.

I asked Jill what timeframe she was looking at for her move from San Francisco to London. She wasn't sure, but she felt like it would be in the next few months. We discussed that *we*, as a couple, would hardly change because of the amount of time I already spent in London. The arrangement would suit my interests but perhaps not hers because of her tendency to nest. Truthfully I would miss our "home-life" and the closeness we had established in Walnut Creek. Jill was by far the classiest, sexiest, and most trustworthy woman I had ever known. The women in my experience rarely had integrity when it came to getting what they wanted and had no regard for the male party involved. Jill was a singular lover and friend, and an unquenchable fire for her burned in my soul continuously.

My workweeks continued, with my taking frequent trips to London and managing the charters as they were sold. My very private "courier" service thrived also. Jill received a raise with her new assignment to International Medical Corps of London and received two months to arrange her move and to select her offices outside London, near Bromley in Kent. Jill made Mrs. Hitler an offer to join her on the move, and thankfully the nanny was keen on moving to England for the adventure, and the increased salary Jill had offered her sweetened the deal. Jill's company had generously included the cost of the nanny, the move, and many benefits she had not had before.

We were excited about the move and had a party with all of Jill's local friends at the Fairmont Hotel in downtown San Francisco. To coordinate with her move, I arranged a trip to London so I could accompany Jill, David, and the nanny to Bromley. We stayed in two suites at the Pan American Intercontinental Hotel, and we were all enjoying the moving adventure. I contacted my Pan Am associates to assist Jill with finding a proper office complex for about thirty employees. Additionally we looked for a residence house near Bromley and found a marvelous old two-story Tudor with two bedrooms on the main floor, a large bedroom upstairs for the nursery, and a cozy upstairs suite for Mrs.

Hitler. The house was approximately 3,500 square feet and was rather large compared to most of the English Tudor houses in the neighborhood.

Jill was so graciously thankful for my help and the help of my Pan Am staff members who dropped what they were doing to assist us on moving day. Within a few days, we had also found Jill a wonderful office space nearby, which had the potential to grow as much as she would need. There would be some travel required in her role as Director, but the travel would be minimal since metro London would keep her quite busy. Dr. Jill Meadows would consult with major hospitals in and around London and with hospitals throughout the English Isles on their management of all medical services and the interactions of the staff with the doctors. Her being an MD made the position all the more attractive and suited to her consulting and management skills.

Her reputation had preceded her, and her expertise was welcomed and utilized right away. The company introduced her at large cocktail party and dinner at the Hotel Dorchester, where over three hundred folks hardily welcomed her aboard. She would spend the next several weeks selecting her staff members with medical backgrounds, nurses, doctors, administrators, and pharmaceutical representatives. Our lives had been turned upside down in less than two months. However, all seemed to be working out well, and Jill was very excited about the advancement and a chance to demonstrate her administrative medical acumen. Jill did not want to sell the house at Walnut Creek or the one in Anacortes. She told me those were ours to use whenever we were in the area, together or separately.

While I was in London, I made several trips around Western Europe and rescheduled my appointments to accommodate my time away from the San Francisco office. I had also been able to make several courier trips for Leo during the side trips. After two weeks I returned to San Francisco. I checked in with Walter Kosky, and my overseas banking accounts now totaled over $3 million and were growing monthly. I continued living in Jill's house in Walnut Creek and continued to work with Pan American out of my base office in San Francisco. Jill wanted me to keep the Walnut Creek house, so I would always have an address and a place to call home no matter where in the world my travels with Pan American took me.

Shortly after returning to San Francisco, I scheduled my first luxury-charter trip to Hong Kong—my first charter to Asia. Leo was appreciative that I would become familiar with the Orient, where, not surprisingly to me, he also had many business contacts. The Hong Kong charter was a jumbo jet with first-class configuration for mostly Asian travelers.

I called Leo from a pay phone at Zack's and advised him of my upcoming trip details and the dates that I would be in Hong Kong. Leo laughed loudly and stated that he had a perfectly matched courier need in that area of his worldwide network. He again reminded me that he would have his staff in San Francisco and in Hong Kong prepare a courier package for my trip over to Hong Kong and also for my return trip back to San Francisco, and he would probably arrange several packages for the side trips I would be taking during the ten-day charter package out of Hong Kong. I had four days to prepare for the trip and make contact with Leo's "messenger" here in San Francisco. The next day I received a phone call advising me to meet Leo's contact at the Top of the Mark bar. I met the "messenger" at noon, and surprisingly she was the redheaded, flirty Iranian beauty from Munich. She grinned broadly and extended her hand for me to shake.

She said, "I thought we'd meet again," but it was certainly a surprise to me. She reminded me that her name was Melina. She looked stunning in an emerald suit and white blouse with her long, red locks swinging as she walked, and she showed off her legs to me so I could clearly see that her figure was magnificent. She said that now that I "had paid my dues" to Leo and was a member of his business family, she could reveal more information to me as we talked. Melina was a puzzle to me. I had my usual Maker's Mark and Heineken, doubles at noon. Melina ordered champagne, and we shared the cashews.

Melina revealed to me that her name was coded at times as Sophia. I wondered if Leo would eventually give me a codename or if I would ever need one for his line of service. Melina knew much more about me than I expected, probably through Leo's network of information specialists. I remember being slightly suspicious of her inquisitive demeanor at our last meeting. Melina said she would slide a briefcase under the table upon our departure, the exact brand of briefcase and color I used all the time. I didn't ask what was in the case but confidentially reaffirmed to her that I would never carry any illegal drugs, as I had told Leo over two years before. She smiled, took my hand possessively in hers, and said that Leo would never involve us with such items. She affirmed Leo's integrity to be solid and that he had assured all his employees, especially the couriers, that no illegal drugs would ever be handled.

I felt a degree of relief that the past two years' worth of couriering for Leo had probably at least been free of illegal drugs. Melina comically indicated that the packages, which I had been carrying for Leo for the last couple of years now, had been the "sparkly" type of items. Melina seemed so knowledgeable about Leo's business that I asked her what she thought my take would be from the current trip. She answered quickly and matter-of-factly that it would be over $2 million. The number two million rolled off her tongue as easily as if she had said "two dollars," but she mentioned that any additional side trips would hike my total well over that amount. Melina asked if I would be able to take a side trip to Tokyo; if so there would be an additional $300,000 for that trip alone. Melina said that one of Leo's agents would arrange "the transfers" for me on all the side trips if I could arrange them while the charter was in Hong Kong.

Melina stood up and left me as surprisingly quickly as she had appeared with only a sassy nod for me over her shoulder as she turned to leave. Melina was still a puzzle to me.

I was pleased that I had developed such an excellent rapport with the customs agents at the San Francisco airport; that would come in handy now. I would not be expecting any inspection of my luggage or my briefcase. The charter day arrived, and the Pan Am 747 was decked out in its usual first-class splendor. Most of the Asian men were Chinese, but a few Japanese businessmen were in the group as well. Their trip was purely business, and they would be enduring twelve-hour days in stuffy, windowless hotel conference rooms. That meant I would not be expected to entertain them during the day, and I could take short day trips to Tokyo and Bangkok for Leo's courier items. The Asian businessmen had their own daily agendas and would not expect to see me again until our trip home.

Upon my arrival in Hong Kong, another attractive woman who identified herself as one of Leo's "granddaughters" met me. I laughed, and we adjourned to the Hotel Peninsula via taxi and went immediately to their wonderfully decorated bar—one of the finest anywhere in the world. We asked for a quiet table in the corner of the bar, away from the crowds of chattering international businessmen. The young woman introduced her-self to me as Niki; I had come to realize that none of Leo's "granddaughters" were ever expected to have last names. She was Eurasian, very intelligent based on her conversation, and smartly savvy in her knowledge of our joint venture. Niki was pretty but not as beautiful as I had come to expect from Leo's "granddaughters." Niki spoke perfect English as well as several dialects of Chinese, Mandarin, and Japanese. She asked me to slide my briefcase under the table, and she slid an identical one toward me. Again, as always, it was a perfect, exact duplicate of my briefcase I had used for years that was exchanged under the table. She stated I was to deliver the case to Tokyo tomorrow. I was already suffering from severe jet lag and lack of sleep and was not looking forward to the early morning flight to Japan. However, for the additional bonus of $300,000, I would endure the trip, smile, and enjoy the coffee as Leo had suggested. I took the Pan American flight 002 around-the-world schedule from Hong Kong to Tokyo. Upon my arrival in Tokyo, again one of Leo's associates met me, a Mr. Motosuka this time. After clear-ing customs, we headed for the bar, and I had my usual Maker's Mark and Heineken. Mr. Motosuka had sake while we smoothly exchanged briefcases under the table; then we made small talk about the weather for about an hour before my Pan Am reverse flight 001 took off back to Hong Kong.

Arriving in Hong Kong, I again met Niki at the Peninsula Hotel bar, and this time we drank lots of booze and shared infor-mation about our businesses. I explained to her that I had to excuse myself to get a power nap or embarrass myself by falling asleep at the bar. I casually passed the briefcase to her. Niki smiled; she knew my schedule better than I did and understood how severely jet-lagged I was. I retired to my room at the Peninsula Hotel and took a nice long shower followed by a nice long six-hour nap. I had room service bring me up a bottle of Maker's Mark and some Kirin beer along with some finger-sized quiche and fresh oysters with hot sauce.

About eight hours later, Niki called and said she had a very important service to discuss with me. I asked her to just join me in my suite for dinner. Niki arrived about ten minutes later, and was dressed to the nines. We shared the ample booze and food leisurely, but "the important topic" was hanging in the air. Finally Niki indicated that Leo required a larger cargo courier service to Bangkok—larger than I was used to transporting. The cargo would require a suitcase in addition to the usual briefcase to transport the weight of the larger shipment. The danger was magnified and sent up a warning flag to my better judgment.

Additionally, arranging the flight from Hong Kong to Bangkok via Pan American schedules would be difficult. I would have to wait until the next day to catch the flight. I asked Niki if all could be in order for the next day's flight. She said haltingly that the next day would give her just enough time to get the shipment ready. I told her that I would expect a much larger bonus for the extra danger this trip entailed. Niki agreed and said that Leo had already authorized an additional $2 million just for this trip because of the significantly increased danger going through customs. The offer included couriering the sparkly stuff both going and coming. I agreed but uneasily this time, with multiple reservations about my own security as well as the shipment's security in Asia, where I was less well known to both sides of the glass in the customs stations.

The next day's flight to Bangkok was smooth, and lots of bourbon calmed my nerves, which were on edge even though I was traveling with Pan Am staff and crew members whom I knew. As

I passed through customs, a Thai customs official stopped me and asked to see my suitcase but not my briefcase. I was stunned by the request and pretended to comply casually. Had Leo's staff done a good job of concealing the hardware? I hoped for my life they had. I myself had never opened any of the cases I had transported.

The customs officer looked me over sternly and then opened the suitcase so slowly that the hairs on my arms stood on end, and I briefly pictured myself rotting in a small Thai prison cell with only bananas to eat for the rest of my life. Loudly he snapped the suitcase shut abruptly and, to my chagrin, motioned for another heavily armed agent to come our way. Maybe I wouldn't even live long enough to see the inside of the small Thai prison cell. Then the agent looked me in the eye and smiled widely, winked, and passed me on through. Over his shoulder, he called to me to give his regards to Leo. Damn!!! Leo's reach was everywhere, and I was covered. I think I exhaled for the first time in thirty minutes.

The return flight back to Hong Kong was uneventful, and I delivered another of my usual briefcases to Niki, who was waiting for me at the Peninsula Hotel bar. I was so relieved, I think I drank more than usual this time, and then I casually passed the new briefcase to Niki before retiring to my room. I was exhausted from the earlier adrenaline rush and the most unwelcome scare at the customs station in Bangkok.

The Pan Am charter group was scheduled to leave Hong Kong and return to San Francisco in four days, and I took the time to do a sentimental journey back to Kyoto, to the little hotel where Jill and I had met. I took the train there and was delighted to reminisce and see many of the places Jill and I had visited while I was recuperating from my war injuries. I telexed Jill almost every day, and she was so happy that I had wanted to return to Kyoto. She wanted to drop everything and join me. I would have truly loved that if she could, but she was so embedded in her new job that time off for her right now would have been impossible. I felt so at peace in Kyoto. I rested there leisurely for the next three days before taking the train back to Tokyo for the return trip to San Francisco with the Asian businessmen. My first luxury charter to the Orient was finished successfully.

The trip back to San Francisco felt like *going home*, but I braced myself and my emotions against the realization that Jill would not be there to meet me at the airport and welcome me home this time. Now that she was in London when I was in Walnut Creek, she felt a million miles away, and I missed her so much more than I had expected to. I carried another new briefcase back with me, but this one was empty for the continuing show and, of course, to be ready for the next exchange. I was glad to get back home to Walnut Creek; Jill's perfume was still there, and my memories drifted into melancholy. There were so many times I relished being alone, but this was not one of them. I simply missed her. Jill still had a very special place in my life and in my heart, but marriage was still out of the question.

13

[JIM HUMMING: "YOUNG GIRL" BY
GARY PUCKETT & THE UNION GAP]

I WAS REWARDED WITH a long-overdue week off after the long
charter trip to Hong Kong, and I decided to fly to Billings,
Montana, and go skiing. I love the feel of the wind on my face, the
fleeting fear in my gut, and the adrenaline rush as I fly down the
advanced ski runs. I was somewhat surprised at myself that I had
not even looked for female company for several days now. I was
having so much fun, and I was just not in the mood to play the
"twenty questions, dinner, and fuck" game.

However, one singular incident captured my curiosity, and I
was embarrassed, at twenty-eight years old, that I loved feeling
nineteen again. A young teenage girl, probably thirteen, at the bottom of the ski run had overtly flirted with me, and I was, of course,
flattered that a young teenage girl would find me attractive. She
made such a "little-girly" show with her winks and flattery that I
finally asked her if she would like to join me for hot chocolate.

She grinned broadly and said, "Yes, of course, Mr. Southerner! I'm Sally!"

I guess my Southern accent from Atlanta had caught her attention. We actually had a grand time talking about Montana, the snow conditions, ski equipment and brands, and the great slopes and runs at Red Lodge. Sally begged me relentlessly to join her and her family for dinner at their cattle ranch that evening. She said it was nearby and thousands of acres, and I couldn't miss it. Sally was so insistent that I finally accepted with strong reluctance and was worried that her parents would find it too too odd for an older man to be invited home to dinner by their beautiful, really young thirteen-year-old daughter.

That evening I took a taxi over to the address she had given me. The house was indeed as she had described—a huge, sturdy lodge surrounded by thousands of acres of ranch land in every direction for feeding cattle. The wide front porch was stacked with cords of cut oak for the massive fireplace inside. As I entered, Sally ran over to me, hugged me, and rambunctiously swung around my neck as both of her embarrassed parents welcomed me and asked Sally to stop bothering me. As we sat by the fire making small talk, as strangers invariably do, another beautiful young woman around eighteen demurely joined us. She was excitedly introduced to me by Sally as her *much older* eighteen-year-old sister. I think I was catching on to Sally's game now.

The eighteen-year-old sister's name was Jody, and I couldn't take my eyes off her. Jody had long, braided blond hair; green eyes that sparkled in the firelight; and a figure that even Hollywood starlets would envy. Her innocent aura captivated me, and I fell in love with the warmth of her presence as she stared into my eyes. The unexpected feeling that hit me was instantly magnetic and the only thing in my life that I have ever experienced that remotely might be construed as "love at first sight," a very foreign feeling to me.

Sally insisted that Jody sit right next to me and squeezed her closely in between us on the hearth of the huge old fireplace. Her father asked me a number of questions about my career. I briefly told him what I did for Pan Am and that I traveled constantly and came to Red Lodge only for rest and relaxation after hectic schedules and weeks of travel connected with work. I was so aware of Jody's body heat against my thigh, it was frightening. Jody stood up, brushing against me so slowly that every nerve in my body was on edge. I watched every molecule of her as she seemed to glide into the large country kitchen to help her mom set the table and finish preparing dinner, but her green eyes stayed glued on me under her long eyelashes. I wondered if she knew how beautiful she was, but she seemed so innocent, so maybe she didn't know that yet. I already regretted the consequences she would endure after she found out.

Jody and I watched each other all evening and enjoyed a wholesome meal of what seemed like every homegrown vegetable on the planet—a meal as wholesome as the entire family seemed to be. It was clear now that Sally had purposefully meant for me to come home with her to meet Jody. After supper Jody took my hand softly and led me into the front parlor, which also had a huge fireplace, and we sat and chatted till almost midnight. The time evaporated into more memories than I can count. My mind was focused on her as if nothing else were on the planet but her, and yes, she beguilingly returned the unlikely connection with her captivating green eyes staring back at me the entire time we were talking.

I told Jody that it was time for me to leave, and she seemed very reluctant to let me go. She walked me to the front door; we embraced tenderly, and she gave me the sweetest, softest kiss on the lips I have ever had...I was stunned and excited all at the same time. The entire family had treated me all evening as if I were nineteen years old, and now I wished a little bit that I was. I returned to my room at the Sheraton Red Lodge and went to sleep after the long day of skiing and the unbelievably "nice", old-fashioned evening. Did I just have my twenty-eight-year-old, very experienced heart stolen by an eighteen-year-old girl?! I was sure with her looks Jody must have had her pick of boyfriends all over Billings since she was born!

Sally did tell me the cold, hard truth the next day on the ski lift. Sally said Jody's "boyfriend" was only nineteen and was very immature for his age; Sally didn't like him, and her parents didn't think he was the right one for Jody either. I was amused that in her naïve little thirteen-year-old brain, Sally did think I was the "right one." The plot was thickening. I had somehow expected that there would be a boyfriend. Jody was bound to have many boyfriends and her pick of the available crowd. I would now have to deal with the unfortunate "boyfriend" situation with a degree of jealousy, and I laughed at myself at the same time. Imagine me, at my age, jealous of a nineteen-year-old teen male?

I could not hold back my admiration for Sally and Jody and their family; they were a true all-American family, full of patriotism, high Christian morals, hard work, and love for all those around them. I had five days left at Red Lodge and happily enjoyed each and every day with Sally and Jody. I developed enough willpower to only kiss Jody good morning and good night. I hurled out of my mind any intentions of trying to seduce her, out of respect for her and her family. The intentions were very much there in my mind, but I was able somehow to subdue the lecher in myself for the remaining few days in Billings. I did imagine that if I were ever to marry, it would have to be a girl just like Jody—natural, innocent, and unbeguiling—and she would have to come from a strong, wholesome, all-American, patriotic Christian family like hers. Marriage was never in any of my realistic plans even for the distant future.

Sally spent a lot of time with us, kind of as a chaperone for her folks, which I truly appreciated in case my resolve were to start faltering. I truly respected the whole family, including her mom and her dad, so much. Respect for Jody's family checked me at every moment when I felt like taking her in my arms and kissing her like she had never been kissed before, and of course my mind always finished the fantasy with just completely seducing her.

Leaving the Billings airport was a mechanical work of art. The runway was on top of a mesa, a flat-top mountain, and it was always a difficult, unnerving takeoff. As we flew out over the edge of the mountain, I could see Jody's ranch lands, and it made me sad and happy at the same time. It had been truly exhilarating and uplifting to experience the innocent, blissful joy that young love is made of. To feel that young again is priceless.

14

[JIM HUMMING: "I ONLY HAVE EYES

FOR YOU" BY THE FLAMINGOS]

As ALWAYS I telexed Jill almost daily from the Northwest Airlines office in Billings. She kept me grounded. Jill was delighted that I took time off from skiing and resting to check in with her so frequently. She had pretty much settled into her new offices and home in Bromley and was making great strides in her new role as Executive Director of Medical Services. She had begun traveling the routes to the hospitals in the British Isles and Scotland. It seemed as though we would be lifelong friends and lovers. My admiration and desire for her was still stronger than any other force in my life, even during our long absences from each another. I checked in with my Pan Am office in San Francisco daily while I was in Billings and also with Walter Kosky, my "overseas broker." I had accumulated almost $5 million dollars over the past two years in my multiple accounts. I had also received telexes from Leo while I was in Billings asking me to "get back on the playing field," saying that business was too good, and that they were overflowing with courier opportunities from all over the world. I telexed Leo back that I was going to London via Miami and would arrive in London the day after tomorrow. I was stopping in Miami just long enough to pick up a courier package that Leo had already instructed me to carry to London using our regular pickup and delivery methods. My usual fee was $300,000. The transfer involved the usual suitcase and briefcase. The courier fee was more lucrative, but the trip was also riskier if a customs official who was not familiar with me challenged me. Usually my Pan American ID and associates rushed me past these guys and the usual customs stations.

Arriving in London, I checked in at the St. Ermin's Hotel and sent my usual Glenlivet outside to Johnny Cain, my baggage-master friend, as my bags were being sent to my favorite room, number 1969, which was the same year I returned from Vietnam. I ordered Maker's Mark and an ice bucket of Amstel Beer along with two dozen oysters and a tray of their fresh-baked miniature quiches. They must have put them in the oven when they saw me check in, or Johnny tipped them off when he saw me arrive.

There was a knock on the door, and there was Mr. Spiros accompanied by a beautiful young woman dressed to the nines, with striking red hair. The girl was another of Leo's "granddaughters" who often accompanied the courier to provide cover for customs officers who were more suspect of singular travelers. We exchanged the booty and enjoyed the St. Ermin's booze and hors d'oeuvres tray. The girl's name was Sherry. Leo's "granddaughters" never used their last names, and I was learning not to ask or ever expect one. Sherry invited me to dinner with her that evening, but I felt obligated to try to catch up with Jill since I was in London. Jill, however, happened to be traveling in Scotland, so I phoned Miss Sherry and told her that dinner would be great. She laughed heartily and chirped, "Yes, it *will* be great because it'll be on Leo's tab!"

I kept Jill's number handy and contacted her after my afternoon nap. Jill was planning to be back in London in two days. This would give me time to see what Miss Sherry had "in store for me." Mr. Spiros had indicated earlier that she was looking forward to being with an experienced man and loved ex-Marines like myself. We met in the lobby bar, where we had several drinks and Beluga caviar with hot toast points and butter. After getting a nice buzz on, we walked over to the hotel's front steps. Johnny, my baggage-master friend, seeing me coming, had already hailed a taxi for us.

Miss Sherry told the taxi driver to take us to the Inn on the Park for our special dinner in the Crystal Room on Leo's tab. We had a feast of caviar, standing rib roast, a medley of fresh regional vegetables, and a tray of fresh breads and aged cheeses from around the world. We had also shared a magnum of Dom Perignon champagne and were feeling no pain at all. I excused myself to the men's room. Surprisingly, once I was inside, Miss Sherry joined me in the room, which was empty except for the female attendant. Sherry took me by my tie and led me into one of the stalls. She took a seat on the toilet stool and unzipped my trousers. She pulled down my pants and underwear slowly but deftly. Kissing my privates, she sent me into hyper erection in seconds. She caressed me and licked me all over before giving me the most excellent head. She expertly wielded the hot liquid from me easily while we listened to the other patrons come and go.

Then it was her turn. I exchanged the seating arrangement with her. She pulled up her designer skirt, unbuttoned her blouse, and took off a gorgeous red-lace brassiere, pressing two very warm melons hard against my bare chest. Off came her red-lace panties and her garter belt. She nimbly lowered herself down on me and inserted my still-stiff shaft far up into her. She was extremely wet, and I could smell the sweetness of her honey. She rode me like a roller coaster until we both finished grandly. We scrambled, helped each other put back on the clothes we had removed, and somehow departed smartly dressed. She gave the expectant attendant a hundred-dollar bill for her silence and for redirecting several curious men away from our stall, which was "active." Miss Sherry put that on Leo's tab also.

Miss Sherry and I returned to my suite at the hotel and slept like babies until noon the next day. We needed the "hair of the dog" when we finally awoke. We adjourned to the fireside café and had bloody marys and omelets for breakfast as we recovered from the previous evening's good food, drink, and kinky sex. Surprisingly my cock was a little sore as I stretched out in the café recliner while still nursing a bloody mary. Sherry appeared to be walking with a little extra care too, and we laughed at our *battle scars* from the night before.

Miss Sherry and I would share a number of rendezvous in the years to come as we worked for Leo and partied heartily together. She and I loved to laugh at the dough we tallied on Leo's expense account across Europe and the Middle East. Sherry became a good friend and pleasant business partner as the years passed. She was only nineteen but a true woman of the world. She left me with my courier bags after two fun-filled days, hugged me, and wished me luck. Sherry purposefully bid me *adieu* before it was time for Jill to arrive back in London.

I met Jill at Heathrow Airport near London. We hugged, had a long kiss, and loved just reuniting again after weeks of being apart. Nothing ever changed with us. The kiss brought us instantly back together, and my lust for her never ebbed. Our conversation was immediately uplifting and fun.

We took a cab back to her house in Bromley. I spent several days there with her, catching up on David and her new job. She was happier than I had ever seen her. She commented that she saw me every time she looked at little David. I enjoyed the home routines, with Mrs. Hitler, the nanny, cooking all of our meals while we played with David.

Jill gave me all the details about her new job and how much business she had established with upcoming clients as the private hospitals were being remodeled and rebuilt. She had projected two new hospitals to be built over the next two years and had hundreds of aging clients who preferred the deluxe accommodations and special treatment at the private hospitals. Her salary and bonuses were approximately $1 million dollars per year and included all of her expenses, the nanny, the house, and a vacation home in the Cotswolds. No one deserved this life more than Jill. She was hardworking, driven, and an extremely dedicated person in both her business life and her personal life with David and me. We made passionate love each evening and early each morning, to the point we woke up the nanny quite often. Mrs. Hitler smiled a lot at breakfast but never spoke a word about our lovemaking.

While out for drinks at the St. Ermin's Hotel, Jill turned very serious about David's upbringing and about his needing a male figure in his formative years. He was now past two and was already seeing his little friends with dads. Jill said she knew *we* wouldn't marry, but that *she* might like to marry in order to fill that void in David's family life. I agreed with her, and she jokingly asked if I had any recommendations? I told her I didn't know of any man on the planet who could possibly deserve her or precious David. She teared up and said how wonderful a family the three of us would make. We held each other tight, both knowing it would not happen. We laughed that someday my future might be bright enough that I could keep her up as she had me. Jill smiled a lovely, melancholy smile, held my hand, and patted it gently. I still loved her more than any other woman I had ever met.

15

[JIM HUMMING: "BORN FREE"

BY MATT MUNRO]

T HE NEXT DAY I departed from the St. Ermin's Hotel in London
with two luggage bags plus another larger briefcase. Leo was
making a major deposit back in New York. The courier fee cut
went up to $500,000.

Arriving in New York City, I checked in at the Pan Am lounge,
where I had my baggage delivered. Again I passed off my baggage
to another courier who had identical baggage and a Pan Am membership in the NY Clipper Club. This was a change in our normal
routine because passing several pieces of baggage plus the suitcase
in the Clipper Club was triply dangerous. The change was necessary due to documents required for the courier going back through
customs. With my luggage tags, which had Pan American ID on
them, he could walk straight through customs without a hassle. It
worked out just fine, but I was more nervous than I had been in a
long time. I'd earned the half-million-dollar cut in spades.

After my courier service in New York City, I returned to San Francisco via Pan Am. I did carry a regular briefcase back to San Francisco with more "ice," but the briefcase looked identical to my normal carry-on, so I was not nearly as uneasy, and the fee was not nearly as much either—only $25,000 for a few hours of stress.

Getting back to my San Francisco Pan Am office the next morning, I was surprised that a party was being thrown in my honor. I was shocked to learn that my boss, Tom Sheff, was suddenly retiring after thirty years with Pan Am; I was next in line to take his place as Director for Luxury Charters, both East and West coasts. I was ecstatic, and my associates, who had obviously known a little bit ahead of me, cheered and welcomed me warmly.

I would be commuting every other week between San Francisco and New York City and spending much more time on the phone and telex. The change in my position of employment meant I would have carte blanche to travel all over the world and would be even more secure from customs agents and gate security as a senior officer for Pan Am. No customs agent would dare consider inconveniencing or even delaying a senior Pan American officer with questions, much less an inspection. The salary upgrade was considerable but paled in comparison to what I was earning with Leo for my courier services. My Pan Am salary went from $65,000 including commissions up to $120,000 plus commissions. The commissions would jump considerably because I now would gain commissions on my own sales as well as the sales made by my team, the twelve major international luxury-charter sales representatives.

My retiring boss, Tom Sheff, briefed me on the status of all the pending charters and asked where I would like to go on my

February and March vacation. I was surprised that I would still have the luxury of two months off now that I was Director.

Tommy laughed and said, "Your new job will give you all the time off you need to rest and relax, and you may even want to join some of the tours that your charter representatives have booked."

Additionally Tommy mentioned that I would now have February, March, and April off to do as I pleased as long as I kept in close touch with the charter representatives and their tours. I celebrated with Tom after the party. We arrived at the Top of the Mark and drank till almost midnight. We talked briefly about any advice he might have for me about my new position. His advice was to spend time with my loved ones and not to travel till I became jaded or "homeless," so to speak. Tom Sheff continued to brief me that it was very easy to travel first class on every scheduled airline in the world, to enjoy all the deluxe hotels and the finest cuisine, and then to stay so busy chasing women all over the world that you forget all about your roots and family. Tom had a beautiful wife and three children, and he was immensely looking forward to finally spending some quality time with them.

Tom was *right on* regarding the "homeless" feeling that I felt traveling so much of my life. The little house in Walnut Creek was just an "address" for me. I told him that I had decided not to marry. Tom knew I loved the women and was somewhat taken aback by my statement. He brushed it off, thinking I just hadn't met the right one yet!

"Never say never," he joked with me. "She's out there somewhere, and you travel enough that you are bound to finally bump into her one day."

"Yes," I retorted cheerfully. "I guess I just want the best of both worlds."

Tom laughed with me again and confided that he had started off that way too over thirty years ago, but the traveling "homeless" life had just worn him down, and he was anxious for the family life in addition to the first-class travel and deluxe hotels. Tom said that he had made a point of taking his wife and three children on most of his latter charter trips and felt like that was the only time he had had with them. I admired Tom Sheff as a boss, a father, and a gentleman. Tommy picked up our entire tab, but his advice was worth a million. Being married with home and family just didn't seem like even an imaginary dream for me right now.

To further celebrate and settle my mind into the new position, I took a couple of days off and traveled to Seattle, where I rented a new Mustang Cobra. I drove on up to Anacortes to check on Jill's house and then on to Victoria, British Columbia. I looked at houses in Victoria and found an old stone manse with acreage surrounding it. The old sturdy mansion had all the things I required: fireplace; large, screened porch and portico; four bedrooms; library; a corner glass-windowed conservatory that I planned to use as an office overlooking the Oak Bay; and a beautiful flower and kitchen garden that was over an acre. I purchased it after looking at half a dozen properties over several days. I was an easy sale from an aging couple who needed the cash. They had priced it at a very modest $250,000, and I paid their full price with no haggling. I later had the property appraised for over $400,000.

I called Walter Kosky, my broker in Amsterdam, and he arranged a wire transfer of cash into my Canadian bank account in Victoria. There were no damn salesmen, lawyers, realtors, or brokers to fuck with…the couple and I happily celebrated together with champagne on the lawn. Weeks later, after closing, I placed the deed and sales papers in a newly opened bank box near the Empress of China Hotel. I then had high tea at the "Empress," went back to my new home, and took a nap. I had bought the house with all the furnishings except for a few smaller sentimental items the older couple wanted to take with them. They were aging and were going to live with family. I loved my new home with all its trimmings. This house belonged to me, so officially I was no longer a "kept man!". I was free!

With my pick of cities all over the world, I just loved the clean, old-world feel of "Vicky," as the locals called Victoria, the small, quaint village in British Columbia, Canada. My money and deed were safe in a bank that Leo just happened to own. With a home and now an address of my own and a secure, legitimate professional position, I felt free—really free! I incidentally learned later that the motto of the city of Victoria is "forever free."

I took the British Columbia ferry from Victoria back to Seattle with my new rented Cobra stowed onboard. I drove out to the small, private cottage Jill had generously bought for us in Anacortes over five years ago. I used my key to go in and check everything out. We had hired a groundskeeper and his wife to keep an eye on it in our absence. All was well, and it brought back so many happy memories of us playing there and enjoying the straits, the fishing, and the excellent, world-renowned fresh salmon, cod, and halibut. The memories of Jill made me think how special she was in my life. She was one of the few people I could trust with my heart and my feelings. She felt like a permanent part of my life. I still had no intentions of marriage to anyone, no matter what my feelings, and then...there were also the secrets of my life that no one would ever know.

16

[JIM HUMMING: "DIAMONDS ARE
FOREVER" BY SHIRLEY BASSEY]

MY FIRST PRIORITY with my new job as the Director of Luxury Charter Sales, East and West Coasts, was to examine each and every salesman's quota ratio and his relationships with his wholesalers. For years I had done what they were doing and enjoyed consulting with them. My own accumulated experiences gave me an intuitive oversight. Supervising them gave me the freedom to travel wherever and whenever I chose, to oversee the salesmen's business acumen and how they related to our loyal charter clients as well as our land-arrangement providers. I focused on Western Europe, the Middle East, and occasionally Asia. The markets for Leo's "product" were primarily these same geographical areas, but India was beginning to show promising demands for our courier services.

While couriering product to London, I stayed at the Inn on the Park, just to change my old habits, break from my years of routine at the St. Ermin's, and hopefully divert any unwanted attention away from my side trips. The upper management expected the younger charter salesmen to experience different hotels, bars, and restaurants in the interest of flawlessly entertaining our luxury-charter clients. Recently I had enjoyed traveling with a young Pan American charter representative named Pete Flemings. He was like my younger self, energetic and totally dedicated to his clients. I was impressed with his witty sense of humor. Traveling with Pete actually made the old, routine trips fun for me again, but I never became jaded, as Tom Sheff had predicted.

Leo called me during one of my non-routine stays at the Inn on the Park in London; I was never surprised anymore that he always knew exactly where I was and what I was doing and with whom. He asked me to join him in Cyprus again for several days. I was excited about a personal visit with Leo and had not been to his private estate in Cyprus now for seven years. We had been able to conduct all our business through phone calls and meetings with his local associates, whom he seemed to have all over the world, wherever I was.

Leo said he had urgent and important new business to discuss with me. His private Gulfstream jet picked me up at Gatwick Airport outside London for the two-hour flight. On my arrival at his compound, I sensed an uneasiness among the staff. I could feel it in the air. I immediately went to my room, showered, and dressed, and soon one of Leo's "granddaughters" greeted me and led me quietly into his private suite. Upon entering, I was shocked to see him quite ill and in bed, with IVs in both arms, medical equipment, and a twenty-four-hour medical staff surrounding him.

He managed a welcoming smile for me and motioned me over to his hospital bed. He then dismissed the nurses and other support staff, so that I sat next to him in privacy. Leo's most private moments always included Avilash, his lifelong Indian servant. Leo told me the story, saying that fifty years ago, when heated disagreements among the cabal's partners had required gunfire and deaths to resolve, he had lost his first wife, the love of his life, a beautiful Greek girl. Back then and today, Leo had an arsenal of weapons capable of solving any of the cabal's internal or external disagreements. Earlier in his life, Leo had been extremely capable of defending himself in any circumstance, whereas today Leo and the other aging partners seemed to rely heavily on their massive bodyguards. Leo's beautiful and peaceful compound was surrounded by an army of casual-looking bodyguards who were well armed and on the ready. I was just starting to imagine why they might be necessary.

Fifty years ago, during the shootout for control of the cabal, Leo had saved Avilash's life by pushing Avi out of the line of fire and taking the bullet himself. As was the Indian custom for Avi's station in life, Avilash had never left Leo's side since. Avi had self-indentured himself to Leo to be his humble and thankful servant for the rest of his earthly life. Avi never traveled with Leo but was always with Leo on the compound and was kindly attentive to Leo's every need.

Leo haltingly continued talking in the room, which was now silent except for the sounds of the medical devices, which seemed to be keeping him alive.

"Jim," Leo said softly, "my active days appear to be diminishing, and my eighty-two years of living life to the fullest have finally caught up with me but unfortunately have never produced a son, not for the lack of trying." He smiled. Then he continued in a barely audible whisper, "I am going to ask you to consider becoming a full partner in my place in all of my enterprises."

Leo confided that it would be up to me to head up the leadership of the cabal and continue to direct the courier-services network, which now extended literally all over the world, in whatever manner I chose, whether I chose to take some of the items myself personally or chose to select, recruit, and train new couriers under my strictest supervision. I knew the absolutely thorough research Leo had done on every facet of my entire life before involving me in his consortium, so I knew he would expect no less thoroughness from me if new couriers became necessary. The monetary take would be in the millions on a monthly basis.

I was stunned by his honesty and his depth of trust in me by offering a non-family member such a position. I would answer directly to his Board of Directors; they were his other four partners. They were strategically spread out around the world. Leo noted that I had accumulated several millions of dollars in my foreign accounts and really didn't need to take on the dangerous courier assignments personally anymore, but that if I did, the rewards would be far beyond my wildest dreams. The meager ten percent cut I had been used to as a courier would now be the other ninety percent net profit as a partner. Leo further stated that he had a "mother fucker" of a project he wanted me to oversee personally. Leo's mind was still an active player even though his body appeared fragile. My curiosity ran wild.

Leo had taken a giant step in couriering his product by making a major purchase in India. The payload would be almost seven hundred kilos of diamonds of the first quality to be delivered to New York City within a few short weeks. Leo asked if I had any ideas on how to move that quantity and weight of product. I told him I would ponder the possibilities and get back to him the next day at breakfast. Leo seemed pleased that my wheels were already turning and saw the twinkle in my eye just thinking about the mental challenge of figuring out ways to move a shipment of this size.

I enjoyed the pool and sauna with a "granddaughter" named Zona. We did make playful love in the pool and also in the sauna. We slept well together that night after enjoying one of Leo's elegant candlelit dinners, which was served to us privately alfresco, but I arose around four in the morning and begin diagraming the logistics of a plan to carry Leo's large payload. As a senior Pan American executive now, I had carte-blanche access to all of the services Pan Am offered to its senior directors. Leo knew my capabilities and knew I would make creative use of all the privileges available to me to carry out his gigantic transfer from New Delhi to the New York City diamond district.

We met for breakfast around seven. Leo had insisted that Avi dress him so he could join me at the table instead of his bedside, but Leo looked very pale and sickly. Leo did eat as good a breakfast as ever, and he smiled, sensing from my broad grin that I had an idea already for him for his blockbuster project. He couldn't hold back his enthusiasm, and his excitement was infectious for both of us.

"Tell me your ideas, Jim. I knew I could depend on you."

I told Leo that I would purchase a new Mercedes Sports coupe in New Delhi and would request his local associates to configure the auto to hold the payload. He laughed out loud and clapped for joy. He said he knew his Jim Gilchrist could solve the problem. Leo exclaimed, enthusiastically as ever, "Yes! I will send my special auto assembly team to New Delhi ahead of you. They will await your arrival and oversee a perfect conversion of the Mercedes."

Then I added, "Once rigged, I will use my Pan Am cargo pass to ship the car and accompany it myself from New Delhi to New York City via Rome and London."

We both laughed at the prospect of successfully moving that quantity and weight of merchandise, and the payoff would be $55 million for the "firm". As the new partner still serving with Leo, I could expect about $5 million for myself just for the courier service and then as a full partner a fifth of the $50 million dollars. The danger was extraordinary considering the Mercedes would have to be weighed and moved through multiple customs stations. The weight of the load would have to be countered precisely by undetectably removing that exact amount of weight from the Mercedes. Additionally my savvy Pan American associates might question my purchase of an auto in New Delhi.

I had scores of concerns regarding the details but would try my best to work them out over the next two weeks. I compiled volumes of notes and researched every aspect of the journey, including lengths of flights, station reps, customs agents, weight of the auto, and a list of Leo's network of associates who might be able to assist me in every city that was a leg of the project. Leo was usually extremely protective of the identities of his high-ranking agents and associates worldwide but now seemed completely trusting and open with me.

Jill had telexed me on Christmas Eve of 1977, asking that I come visit her and David, again whom I hadn't seen in several years now. I telexed her back early in '78 that I would plan an extended visit with her and David during my three-month sabbatical from Pan American during February, March, and April. The months off would allow me to cover my story about getting a great deal on a new Mercedes Sports coupe in India. My Pan Am associates would understand the trip to New Delhi to procure the car and then envy and respect my purchase of such a fine automobile.

I made up my mind to accept Leo's proposition to be the fifth partner in full, now without the constant consultations with him, and I wanted to prove myself to the entire board of partners by accepting the prodigious Mercedes project, even with the excessive danger associated with the venture. I had evidently gained Leo's complete trust for him to ask me to take his place as the fifth full partner and to complete his swan-song Mercedes project for the cabal. Leo had been my rock during our seven years working together. Now it was my turn to return the favor to an ailing man to whom I literally owed everything.

17

WHILE PLANNING THE Mercedes project, I took several days off to rest and catch up on my sleep. Sleeping at Leo's compound was like heaven on Earth—very quiet and peaceful. I slid easily into Zona more than once. She was always hot and wet and ready. I assumed she was paid handsomely to be at my beck and call. Leo knew well that men of power have needs. I spent most of my time resting and working on the details of the project, but Zona was always nearby if I wanted company.

One night while I was sleeping, I had one of the reoccurring unnerving "flashbacks" of my Vietnam War experiences. The dream was so realistic, I thought I was reliving the war in vivid detail. I had served with the 3rd Marines near the Vietnamese DMZ. I truly believe my war experience was one of the reasons Leo originally chose me as a junior partner, since he himself had served in combat and knew the depth of human trauma a person can experience and the pressures one can endure to survive during mortal combat.

The flashback nightmare was my reality at this moment. The hairs on my neck were standing on end. My breathing was rapid and shallow, and my heartbeat was racing. Many of the young men who entered the Marine Corps during the Vietnam War were from very poor or dysfunctional families. There were only a handful of Marines who had grown up in traditional middle-class families. For the poorer fellows, the Marine Corps was an opportunity to escape their environment, physical abuse from family, and a bleak blue-collar future. My Navy medical training and also my Marine Field Medical School training were considered to be the best trauma school training regimens in the world. We were warned over and over not to become "close" to any of these "grunts." Developing close ties to the guys would invariably distract us from our rigid medical protocols and treatments if they were to become wounded, or if they became psychotic due to combat trauma.

Private Bailey was one of my "exceptions" to the strict training rule. I let Bailey into my heart and mind, and now, years later, he is still a frequently appearing character in my combat nightmares.

Private Bailey was a lean, strong, medium-built young man. He was only seventeen years old and had to have his mother sign a release allowing the Marine Corps to induct him under the age of eighteen. His father and grandfather had both died of black-lung disease from working in the coal mines of West Virginia. Bailey's mother, brothers, and sisters lived in a very modest box house built cheaply by the coal company. Even their sustenance came from "the company store."

Several weeks before Christmas of 1968, our platoon was on a "search-and-destroy" mission around the Quai Viet area of

Vietnam, just south of the DMZ. After a long day of "humping" the bush, our platoon set in for a night perimeter, and we took turns eating our evening meal while the other grunts watched for our enemy, the NVA, North Vietnamese Army, or Viet Cong. I was sitting apart from the others when Private Bailey joined me, and we sat together quietly, eating from our CRATS, (C rations). As we finished our meals from the cans and packages, Bailey asked me a question that all of us had on our minds and were continually thinking about.

"Doc, are you afraid of dying out here so far away from your home and family?" Bailey stated the profound out loud. We never talked about our own personal deaths; that was the forbidden, haunting subject to most of us. What should I tell this young Marine?

"Yes, I am, Bailey. I am afraid of dying here so far from my wife, my family, my friends, and especially my twenty-month-old daughter, Susan Michelle."

Bailey's next comment took my breath away. He said, "Doc, there's something I'm afraid of worse than just dying here."

It took me several breaths to consider his statement. What could possibly be more tragic than dying in a hostile jungle fifteen thousand miles from home and loved ones? Fighting and dying uselessly in a war no one back home even wanted? I braced myself before asking Private Bailey, "What could be worse than dying here?"

He said, "Doc, my biggest fear is dying alone here…with no one around me when I die."

After all the years of medical training and physical preparedness, I was caught totally off guard by Bailey's confession. I wondered how many of the other Marines had that same thought, and how would, should, and could I answer him now and them later? The question was heavy in the air, and we both became very quiet. He looked up at me with sad, searching eyes, but a great calm seemed to come over him. Perhaps because I was older and educated and had been well trained by the Marines and Navy ... maybe that was how he got the courage to express his feelings, and maybe that was why he thought I would have answers for him.

"Bailey," I sighed, "I will be there when you are wounded or dying...you won't be alone."

"But what if you're not there with me and are taking care of our brothers?" he persisted woefully.

"Bailey." I tried to sound strong and decisive for him. "It is most likely I'll be there with you...I can take care of most of y'all based on the severity of the wounds received." This was my own personal greatest fear: deciding, under fire, who should be treated first, who should live, and who should be left to die. "If for some reason I can't be there with you, Bailey, God will be with you."

Normal hospital triage would take the direst emergency cases first. "Field triage" was the opposite. We were taught to save the savable first. The field triage training called for identifying and treating those who could be saved and treating them first and putting off those who appeared beyond saving. Hard to do...

Upon awakening, I begrudged the interrupted sleep. I had been told that these vivid dreams of the war and combat would never go away. The nightmare about Bailey stuck with me, as did several other horrific nightmares that have "stayed around" for years. The nightly episodes visited me intermittently like strange old friends. To escape the reverie, I began meticulously focusing on Leo's Mercedes project. Leo had arranged for all the key players to meet in Rome and go over the details in minutia that would surreptitiously import a half-billion dollars' worth of diamonds into New York City.

18

[Jim humming: "Oh, Lord, Won't You Buy Me a Mercedes Benz?" by Janis Joplin]

Leo's private jet had wheels up at 5:00 a.m. for my flight from Cyprus to Rome. Aboard other planes heading to Rome were his senior partners, each specializing in various aspects of our courier services. The partners all took separate taxis from the private landing strip and planned to have all of their support operatives meet us later in the afternoon. We all arrived in Rome just before lunch and checked into The Grand Hotel. The meeting was to take place in Leo's customary three-bedroom suite with its private meeting room. The hotel staff would send up an elegant but simple lunch for us with Campari and soda.

When the support staff arrived midafternoon, we began the detailed review of the plans and a verbal review by each key person in our entourage. We went over maps, plane diagram configurations, security at the airports that the Mercedes and our team would travel through, local trusted contacts, and the schematics of the Mercedes itself. The diamonds would be undetectable, even to the trained suspicious eyes of the international customs agents. The details were well outlined, and all the key players would work with their local staffs to complete the job. Leo was absent only in body. He wanted to be apprised of every detail. Each of the key players would memorize and repeat their roles, and then we would burn any written documents and plans in the suite's fireplace.

The meeting was successful. No overwhelming problems appeared; however, we knew that we'd all have to be prepared for the unexpected along the way and keep in close communication with each other. The plane route would depart from New Delhi, then head to Rome, then to London, and finally to New York City. The task was herculean but doable. We ordered a dinner fitting to our endeavors, enjoyed magnums of champagne, and retold the good old stories of our past exploits. Leo had known these fellas for over fifty years, and many served in the war with him. To say "trust was important" would be a gross understatement.

In my thirties, I was definitely the youngster of the group, yet I felt accepted and respected for my own previous accomplishments, successes, and self-confidence as well as for my impeccable appearance and dress. Backing all that up, I had Leo's public announcement to all the fellas that I was his "chosen one" to lead the group.

Our meeting in Rome was scheduled to last three days to conduct our business and to hash through all the necessary but tedious details of the logistics of our project; Leo did schedule us one free day off from meetings. Leo knew fresh minds think better. While in Rome on my free day, I met with Mike Blake, one of the Pan Am luxury-charter sales reps who worked for me, and we reviewed the details of his upcoming charters and land arrangements. The meeting gave me just cause to be in Rome for my

Pan Am travel records and the expense report process. Mike was quite young and reminded me of myself at twenty-five: confident, with a penchant for details of every aspect of his charters, so that the clients were given the best possible tours and attention. He was good.

We enjoyed drinks and shared frivolous risqué anecdotes of our previous sexual conquests and the women who remained in our memories. No names were ever mentioned. Over the past few years, I noticed that I had begun humming musical oldie tunes from my past that coincided with current events and my frame of mind. While chatting with this young charter rep, I was humming under my breath the old classic by Frank Sinatra, "Summer Wind." Our stories recalled dozens of women we had met, slept with, and enjoyed life with in our midtwenties. Most men are striving to find *the* "Summer Wind" woman, but my personal position was to put that off until further in my future, if ever. And for now I did love the looking!

I was satisfied with my current bevy of ladies. I had even sent Jill a telex to let her know that I had not forgotten her invitation to me to visit her and David in London. The young sales rep and I parted company at one of my favorite bar and cafés in Rome, the Caffé Greco, in the heart of the Spanish Steps. I thought about the many years of repetitive routine travel ahead for Mike and the small compensation he would receive for it from Pan Am in comparison to my accruing fortune, thanks to Leo.

To accomplish the Mercedes project, I had notified my Pan American office that I would be out of touch for two weeks. I had all my credentials on the ready, including the first-class air passes on major world airlines. Our initial target flight was Pan American's around-the-world flight number two, which matched our plans to the tee. I had arranged the transport of the Mercedes with the Pan Am cargo staff, so that the car would pass through the same airports as I would but at slightly different times. I would inspect the Mercedes at every stop and pick it up finally in New York City.

I departed for New Delhi the next day and arrived in time to be picked up by the chauffeur of Leo's chief courier. We drove about twenty miles outside the city until we came to the remote village where the Mercedes was stored. Leo's specialized automobile crew had meticulously taken out the overhead liner, the seats, and the dashboard. The trunk space was hollowed out so that the car now had ample room to stow away our booty. The diamonds were delivered that afternoon via a large armored van, and the crew labored several hours filling the spaces provided for the cargo. The openings were then sealed shut, and the auto was checked out once again for mechanical roadworthiness and perfect weight. No mistakes were allowed. All the hard work and weeks of preparation had paid off. Now I was on center stage to accompany the cargo transport and deal with any roadblocks along the way personally.

I knew the customs station manager in New Delhi, and we had drinks while the car was loaded into the giant cargo plane headed for Rome. He congratulated me on my choice of cars, and we laughed at the prospect of my riding in the cargo plane to "protect my baby." I left for the New Delhi airport several hours after the Pan Am cargo plane took off. My heart was beating wildly at the undertaking and the possible dreadful consequences to my decision. Even $200 million dollars in courier fees did not make the going great ... yet.

I arrived in Rome several hours after the cargo flight arrived. I walked over to the cargo plane and inspected the Mercedes carefully. Everything was in order, and I signed off on the employee transport papers that allowed me to send my personal auto on its way to London. I wasn't concerned too much about the customs officials in London since I knew the cargo director, John Nesbitt, and had already telexed him to join me for drinks when the car arrived. I met with John a few hours before the car arrived at Heathrow Airport in London. We had drinks and an early dinner and discussed Pan Am business and the selection of my new wheels. He joked with me that now that I was Senior Director of Charter Sales East and West Coasts, I probably had the bucks now to afford a Mercedes.

I offered to show the auto to John, and he accepted my invitation. We walked over to the hanger together, and all the key personnel who worked for John greeted us. The auto had been taken off to provide space for other shipments in front of it. John sat behind the steering wheel and grinned. For these few seconds, the Mercedes was his. He glanced in the backseat and the trunk and congratulated me on my choice. He was green.

We shook hands, and John departed for his office. About an hour later, I watched intently as the Mercedes was loaded back into another cargo aircraft headed for New York City. Then I walked over to the passenger terminal to take the next Pan Am flight to New York City myself. This leg of the journey held the greatest danger. While I knew the key Pan Am personnel in the New York terminal, the Federal customs agents there were always an unknown and unpredictable. Even with all of our meticulous planning, the project could crumble in New York City.

After seven hours on the flight to New York, I waited impatiently on the inside and casually patient on the outside for the cargo plane to land and the Mercedes to be unloaded. I arrived early to see who was checking the manifest and was happy to learn that several of my old buddies would be handling the process, checking off the paperwork, and clearing the auto to enter the United States. The Federal customs agents were mostly unfamiliar to me, but there were several I did know, and I shook hands with them. They smiled enviously and mused about how much I must have saved buying the car in India from an English Baron and then having it shipped to the United States at employee cargo rates. The actual employee savings for shipping the car was about $3,000.

The auto was pulled into the garage just off the tarmac, and the formalities of the Federal customs inspection were started. My Federal agent friend laughed and told the other agents to go over the car quickly, that I probably had a beautiful redhead outside waiting for "a ride." We all laughed together, and the car passed through without any close inspection at all. I breathed out, rolled my eyes, and then drove the Mercedes to the outer gates of the JFK airport and onto the freeway toward Joe Franko's, Leo's contact in New Jersey. I pulled the Mercedes into the large garage of an estate well off the main highway. Upon my arrival several of Leo's very relieved local associates greeted me heartily. They had the best champagne and Beluga caviar waiting on me to celebrate our successful project.

Leo had instructed me to give the keys to the new Mercedes Benz, after it was unpacked of course, directly to his top agent, Joe Franko. Leo was always especially appreciative to Joe Franko because over the years, Joe had been instrumental in liquidating huge quantities of diamonds for Leo in the New York City diamond district. I assumed giving the keys to Joe was Leo's way of thanking Joe, or perhaps it was a gratuity or maybe even "his share." Joe and I and a few of the crew just continued to enjoy the champagne and caviar while the Mercedes's payload was meticulously retrieved in full. I finally handed the keys over to Joe, but to my surprise, Joe just shrugged and said, "It's just work for me," and I saw no jealousy in the eyes of Joe's associates. I was to learn later that Joe Franko, Leo's top agent, would immediately drive the beautiful new Mercedes to the junkyard and would wait to witness it being "crushed" with his own eyes to prevent the FBI, CIA, FAA, or any other government entities from having any link or proof that the "Mercedes project" ever existed.

I was extremely mentally exhausted from stress and lack of sleep during the trip and tired from hours of flight time and hours of wait time. I was determined to treat myself to a long, uninterrupted overnight sleep with no alarms at the end and then call my New York City friend, Gail, with the red Yankee's hat and swinging blond ponytail.

19

[JIM HUMMING: "NEW YORK, NEW YORK" BY FRANK SINATRA]

I CHECKED INTO THE Plaza around 6:00 p.m., into an elegant suite with plenty of Maker's Mark, ice, and fruit and a breathtaking view of New York City. I called my Yankee-hat friend, Gail, and she was thrilled that I was in town. I indicated to her that we wouldn't need her sugar daddy's digs; I was staying in a suite at the Plaza. I got hot just thinking about her coming over and about her coming, period. I had a number of Maker's Marks and an hors d'oeuvres tray delivered to the room in expectation of my blond-ponytailed friend.

She arrived dressed shockingly spectacularly. No red Yankees hat and pony tail this time. As I remembered, she had a voracious appetite and began eating everything in sight, including me. We undressed each other and glided down into the huge whirlpool bath. With the hot, bubbling water swirling all around us, we fucked our brains out. After the wild, crazy sexual interlude, we went to bed totally satisfied and slightly drunk, still tingling from the Maker's Mark and great sex. We slept luxuriously through most of the morning, but when Gail awoke she unabashedly told me she was dressing hurriedly to go home and pack for a four-day vacation in Europe with the sugar daddy. And so it goes with casual sex.

I called Walter Kosky, my financial liaison to Leo, and asked when the dispersion for the Mercedes project would be processed. He advised me that it would take about two days to completely liquidate the cargo into funds. I asked that my funds be deposited equally into the accounts I had on file. Walter asked if I wanted any portion of my payment in diamonds, and I declined, preferring cash. He understood and calculated that my share of the transaction should be deposited into my accounts within forty-eight hours.

I had two days left to play around in New York while my blond Yankee friend was on vacation in Europe with her sugar daddy. Gail said he kept her up, and she had to pay her dues. I called Margo Rosen, an old and trusted contact at an exclusive high-end escort service, and told her I wanted a beautiful red-head who loved to dance and party. I told Margo I would need her for at least two days, and that I preferred a girl with a good sense of humor who loved to laugh at jokes—my jokes, of course—and funny anecdotes. Margo came through with a knockout—a twenty-two-year-old redhead who was tall and had legs all the way up to her chin. Her name was "Ruby," and she had green eyes and a terrific sense of humor. We greeted each other warmly, and it seemed that we'd get along just fine. She verified her fee of $3,000 per twenty-four-hour day, which I had already agreed to with Margo.

The next two days were wonderful, casual, relaxed, and hot when needed. We were not acting like the "business deal" which we were both part of. The natural casualness and poise of Margo's girls were Margo's trademarks for her top clients. The paid experience let me escape the "twenty questions, dinner, and fuck" evenings I usually had on the road. Margo's girls always kept the chase from becoming boring, and they never engaged in any of the bullshit that transpired at the end of so many of my one-nighters on the road.

I checked on my accounts at the banks, and the $200 million was deposited as promised. I now had accumulated about $350 million. Leo asked if I could return to Cyprus to celebrate and to talk some business. I agreed, since I still had vacation days left. I did check with my senior charter sales rep to see if everything was running smoothly and had a brief conversation with my boss, who congratulated me on my new car. He noted that with my shipping charges waived, I could probably sell the car for three times what I paid for it. I told him I had considered selling the fancy Mercedes and buying two new sporty Ford Mustang GTs or GTOs. He said all was well at home and to enjoy the rest of my vacation.

My pro girlfriend, "Ruby" asked if she could join me on my upcoming trip to Cyprus for gratis. There was no pressure for sex, "high maintenance" attention, or nagging from this gal. I agreed to take her with me after checking with Leo. I picked up two first-class passes, and off to London we went.

Arriving in London, we went to the St. Ermin's Hotel, to my usual suite of rooms. I showered and called the spa to schedule a double deep-tissue massage in our room before sleeping—yes, just sleeping. The next morning we ordered a breakfast of eggs Benedict, champagne, and a large tray of strawberries and assorted fruits. "Ruby" was delighted to take an exotic vacation away from Margo's service and was pleasantly surprised that the level of luxury was much higher than she had expected. Ours was the perfect relationship between a man and a woman; take what you want sexually, but don't nag and don't depend on the other for maintenance. "Ruby" was a perfect travel companion in every way.

20

"RUBY" AND I napped at the St. Ermin's Hotel in London, and Leo's limo picked us up en route to his private plane at Heathrow Airport. The short day layover was a refreshing retreat for us both. "Ruby" was so curious and excited about her adventure going to Cyprus that she walked the aisles of the plane repeatedly; I laughed at her girlish, adventurous nature.

We arrived in Cyprus at Leo's estate at 8:00 p.m. and were led to our room immediately. "Ruby" retired early after the long trip, but I felt refreshed after a shower and had a private dinner with Leo. I was humming the song by Crosby, Stills and Nash called "Southern Cross." "Ruby" had turned my head but not my heart, and the song seemed to fit my feelings for her. She refreshed my sense of fun and freedom from dealing with expectations, wants, and things. The grand love of music that I had in my heart often diminished the lack of comfort I sought from any woman. Sometimes the music was just good company enough by itself.

Leo Halaby hugged me grandly for one who appeared so feeble. Avilash had helped Leo dress and come to the table. We shared a light meal of fresh-caught blue-fin tuna, fresh vegetables from his kitchen garden, and fresh fruit from his orchards. No drinks were offered. One should live to be a hundred eating like this.

After dinner I had to ask Leo why he desired my return to his estate so soon. Leo hesitated, his forehead wrinkled, and his eyes became very cloudy. His face and entire demeanor became serious. Slowly, he bluntly told me that his health was failing much quicker than he had expected, and his doctors had admitted to him that he had only a few months left to live. The doctors were wise to allow a man of Leo's incredible intellectual faculties to have time to settle his own estate. I was saddened and stunned by the news. Leo was not only a business partner but also a close friend and "Dutch uncle" to me. He had generously made me a very rich man and had set me free from any financial woes in the future.

Leo was actually comforting me when I should have been the one comforting him. He obviously had had more time than I had to process and become comfortable and serene with his plight. He told me he was approaching eighty-five. He confided in me that his four worldwide partners wanted an extremely trustworthy fresh, young partner to take over his role in their international businesses, and they wanted Leo to begin the process of turning over his duties prior to his becoming incapacitated and too sick to enjoy his last days. Leo smiled slowly and told me that I was his choice, a trustworthy young man without reproach. His four partners trusted Leo's judgment explicitly, but all four of them wanted to meet with me individually. The partners were strategically located in London, Amsterdam, India, and China. I informed Leo that I had only a few days left of my long vacation, but that I could easily manage trips to London and Amsterdam on my way back to San Francisco. And while in San Francisco, I could arrange to join West Coast charter trips to China and India. Leo was delighted and chuckled as he told me there would be a bonus for my being chosen as the fifth partner. I didn't inquire about the reward but knew it would be hefty, along with my usual courier fees.

Leo asked that he might retire after such a long day. As we were leaving, Leo congratulated me on my choice of companions and said he was especially appreciative of just watching "Ruby" walk through his gardens. He stated again that she was stunning and had a very captivating face and demeanor. He joked quickly about the futility of relationships for men like us and suggested once again that I avoid being tied up with anyone who must be fed! I laughed and told him I understood and had avoided being tied down with any woman and had also avoided having a family... Family?! Thoughts of Susan Michelle and David jolted my brain to retract that last statement to Leo, and I did but not out loud. We hugged and said our good evenings to each other, and silently and instantly Avi appeared to assist Leo to his chambers. The news Leo had revealed would dramatically alter both our lives in the very near future.

"Ruby" and I spent the day water skiing and relaxing on the spectacular cabana-sprinkled beaches on Leo's estate. The furnished cabanas with beach service provided privacy for any kind of activities we wished to engage in, and we did them all.

Leo's offer kept me thinking constantly about the pros and cons of being an international partner in his ancient, old-world cabal. The market capitalization for the consortium was over $70 billion dollars now, and Leo would continue to hold the greater portion. I assumed Leo would leave huge sums to his daughter and "granddaughters" but later learned that years ago Leo had made provisions for his "heirs" through a separate trust administered by his banks in London and Amsterdam.

"Ruby" and I packed up at the end of the day in paradise and prepared for our trips back to our respective home bases, she to New York City and I to San Francisco via London and Amsterdam. "Ruby" hugged me fiercely. We were both pleased and smiling, but no future rendezvous with each other was even mentioned.

21

[JIM HUMMING: "ZORBA, THE GREEK"

BY MIKIS THEODORAKIS]

WHEN I ARRIVED in London, Leo had already arranged a meeting for me with one of the four other partners. I rehearsed my résumé over and over in my head. The first partner's name was Demos Mikos, and Leo had told me that the man had a remarkable photographic memory, a superior head for numbers, and the cleverest strategies of anyone for acquiring and processing large amounts of money.

We met in my suite at the St Ermin's. Mikos entered my suite accompanied by a formidable bodyguard and a delicate-looking female associate who acted as his secretary. She was all business, tailored like a librarian, and very intelligent based on her verbal contributions to our introductory statements. Mikos was in his early seventies, a lean, tanned gentleman of Greek ancestry. He had been educated at Cambridge and had headed a number of small companies in his early twenties that became extremely successful. That was when Leo had hand picked him for the cabal.

Mikos had worked his way up in the Greek shipping business and later in the international travel wholesale business. Mikos had read a scanned version of Leo's handwritten letter of recommendation of me, which evidently included quite a thorough résumé of my activities. Mikos seemed extremely impressed with Leo's high opinion of me and my skills. Over strong coffee Mikos and I spent several hours exchanging ideas. We were both anxious for the consortium's business to improve its bottom line. The tight control of such an empire was imperative. Mikos related that he had started with the cabal fifty years ago under the fine direction and leadership of Leo, but that the empire had continued to expand beyond his wildest dreams as a young man. In the present the partners aspired to clearing more than $100 billion dollars over the next three years.

Mikos scrutinized my opinions and body language very carefully when he broached the next subject. He impressed upon me that none of the partners had absolutely any interest or desire to enter the illegal drug business. I seemed to have passed Leo's and his judgment regarding this topic. I had never opened any of the courier cases, but I had taken Leo at his word that none of the cases ever contained illegal drugs. The international conglomerate wanted to continue to focus on diamonds, gold, silver, and cash investments in energy. Mikos did note that India and China were potentially rising profit centers, but that our current geographics continued to generate the majority of the business.

The conversation went circular between business, my military training, my travel experiences with Pan Am, and the women in my life. Mikos was very thorough. He had surmised correctly that I loved the company of beautiful, intelligent women and was careful to warn me about not mixing female relationships with our business; he encouraged me to avoid marriage and to avoid becoming overly entangled with women, especially during courier missions. Mikos knew my reputation and complimented me on keeping my business and pleasure at an arm's length away from each other.

We spent the next six hours exchanging ideas while he continued to evaluate my potential as the full fifth partner. I was encouraged with the genuine smiles he gave me, and his secretary seemed very pleased that he was pleased. We agreed to break and order room service for dinner. Mikos left me to order. I ordered four salads with fresh salmon, fruits, strong coffee, and a light white wine. The group seemed happy with my choices.

After dinner Mikos stood and said that he had been impressed with my résumé and persona and would continue conferring with the other partners. Mikos also said my confirmation was well on its way, promoted by Leo's handwritten résumé and recommendation. Obviously the four other partners looked to Leo as the leader of their future operations. Leo had always been on the lookout for younger men to assume the massive responsibilities of the industry they engaged in. I felt good about my meeting with Mikos but felt slightly more nervous about the upcoming meetings with the other three partners.

22

[Jim humming: "The Good Life" by Tony Bennett]

T HE MEETING WITH the second partner was to be held at the Hotel Okura in Amsterdam. I took the short flight over from London to Amsterdam and checked in to my room, an executive suite with a sitting room, wet bar, and small kitchenette. While in my suite, I called each of my key Pan Am charter sales reps and my Pan Am boss and brought everyone up to speed on sales and the tour status of all of our major accounts.

Jill was always on my mind and in my heart, but I hadn't been in touch with her for several years now and was hungry just to hear her voice and catch up on her life in England married to Jake Samples, the ambassador's administrator. I reached her by phone at home. Mrs. Hitler had taken David for a walk in the park. Jill and I had a wonderfully long catch-up conversation. She indicated her relief in hearing from me, knowing I had been swamped with the international business issues. She still knew only of my position with Pan American Airlines, as the Director of Luxury Charter Sales. I promised her a long weekend soon.

After I finished meeting with the second partner in Amsterdam, I planned to return to London and spend several days with Jill. It appeared that Jake Samples had not been the father to David that she had hoped for; her marriage to the Embassy officer was short lived and had come to a mutually peaceful end. Jill was still excited to see me again and for me to see our son, David, from a distance. Our conversation was wonderfully romantic, and we spared no passionate words. We were both looking forward to renewing our relationship, reminiscing through all our old memories, and just simply being with each other again in person.

The next morning the city central of Amsterdam was bustling with the noise of streetcars and horns honking. The front desk staff called and said, "Mr. Jim Gilchrist, there is a Niko Sebastiaan here to see you, and he requests that you meet him in the bar."

That is my kind of guy. A few drinks before the business portion of our meeting would be a good relaxing first step. He introduced himself to me as Niko Sebastiaan and was also accompanied by a stalwart bodyguard who remained only a few steps away from us. At 11:00 a.m., we decided to have bloody marys in the bar before ordering dinner to be served at one to the three of us in my suite upstairs. The bodyguard watched me closely for almost an hour before he seemed comfortable that I meant his master no harm; however, he continued to be on high alert regarding the people around us and the surroundings. I wondered at what point the danger in my own life, as the new fifth partner, would escalate to the point that I myself would need a bodyguard.

Niko chatted on and on about Leo and how far they went back together. He asked my opinion of Leo and his current health, since I had seen Leo so recently. I assured Niko that Leo's mind was still as intact as ever and that Avilash was an invaluable aide with Leo's increasing frailty. Niko and I got along well and had developed a mutual respect for each other and a familial rapport which had given me a keen insight into the future that Leo envisioned for the conglomerate. Niko indicated that he knew Leo had chosen me partially due to my view of a more robust future for the consortium by seeking further diversification and by updating our contact infrastructure.

After several more bloody marys, we adjourned to my suite for dinner without the bodyguard. Niko Sebastiaan must have felt secure enough with me that he decided the extra protection was no longer needed. The bodyguard lunched just outside in the hallway and waited on Niko dutifully just outside of the door. Niko and I settled into the smartly appointed suite with its small wood-burning fireplace already lit and began a long narrative concerning the details of my vision for the future of the business. We had no name for the project but started calling it "future-istics" just for convenience. Future-istics was taking on its own constantly evolving set of collective ideas. In limited detail I formulated the outline of my vision for our new business ventures, and Niko commented freely and took voluminous notes in Dutch. The meeting was both productive and bonding, and I truly enjoyed the company and charisma of Niko Sebastiaan. He was aging, but the sharpness of his brain and intellect led me to believe that there were still many good years ahead for him with the consortium before the partners began searching for a younger candidate to replace him.

An impeccable waiter served our lunch in my suite on a linen tablecloth. He served us an appetizer of braised eel, fresh salmon, small rocket salads, an assortment of local root vegetables, and Verdicchio, a mildly sweet wine that we both enjoyed. Niko seemed impressed and complimented me on my selection of both food and drink. During the dining hour, we discussed more casual topics and our personal preferences in women, travel, money, and all the small-talk topics two worldly men would discuss in the beginning of a new relationship. Niko indicated that my next two interviews would be in Hawaii, with the two remaining partners representing China and India. Niko confided in me that they had chosen the Hawaiian location for their meetings with me because they wanted the opportunity to spend both business time and ample leisure time with me during their examination.

Niko Sebastiaan left in the late afternoon. We shook hands and agreed that the meeting was a success. He collected his bodyguard, and I walked out with them, watching as the two men walked away into the gray skies and cold winds off the North Sea that Amsterdam is famous for.

From the warmth of bar's fireplace, I called Jill in London. We caught up on small talk, and I asked her if she was sure she still wanted the four-day rendezvous we had discussed a few days ago. When I mentioned my arrival in London the next day on an early Pan Am flight, she squealed with delight. We both knew it would be nothing but happiness to have four long days together. We both wanted plenty of time together and time for me to "see" David, our son, even at a distance. After I hung up from talking to Jill, I relaxed with several bourbons and made the arrangements for my flight back to London and my stay at the St. Ermin's Hotel, in my usual suite.

23

[JIM HUMMING: "YOU MAKE ME SO VERY
HAPPY" BY BLOOD, SWEAT, AND TEARS]

I ARRIVED AT THE St. Ermin's Hotel in London late in the morning and sent the usual Glenlivet out to Johnny Cain, who always took especially good care of my baggage. Of course I went to straight to my favorite bar. There was no one else in the bar, so I joined in a good-natured repartee with the waitstaff and bartenders, who were all familiar. It was too early for bourbon, so I ordered a Campari and soda. I began to relax in the warmth of the fire the staff made just for me. Sitting there at the St. Ermin's at a table next to the fire and waiting on my "baby" to arrive seemed just like old times.

Jill finally appeared, entering through the side brass-and-glass door that had direct access to the bar. We embraced each other tightly, frozen in the moment, and held on to each other like crazy. It was perfect holding her again. When we finally sat down, I noticed that Jill was teary eyed at our embrace. We sat for several moments, just staring at each other. Our souls were in heaven just to look at each other again, clinging to each other's hands and kissing each other's fingertips. The moment was running in slow motion, as if we were trying to capture all of our lost time together and renew the depth of our love.

No other woman ever affected me to the core like Jill did.

Jill loved that we sat at our usual table by the fireplace, and the fire blazed and crackled just for us. I ordered Taittinger champagne; the best seemed the only perfect choice for our reunion. We both laughed and smiled and chatted through a second bottle. At fifty-one years old, Jill looked as beautiful as she had when I'd fallen in love with her twelve years earlier, in 1968, at the Naval Hospital in Yokosuka, Japan. The extra years had only enhanced her attractiveness to me. Over our eight years of separation, I had made love to numerous other women, but Jill continued to be the only one I could never resist. I always felt drawn to her beyond my control. Her figure, her sense of humor, her smiles, her wit, her voice, her frowns, and her persona were what I loved. She was as near perfect a woman as any man could expect...and, incredibly, she *loved me.*

After finishing the second bottle of bubbly, we adjourned to my suite, where another smaller fireplace beckoned us with its warmth and flickers of firelight. The fire was crackling and spitting and smelled sweetly of aged and dried oak burning. The blazing fire paralleled the heat in our souls for each other. We stood in front of the fireplace and kissed passionately for innumerable minutes. Time and Earth disappeared. Jill and I both craved each other and were anxious to "catch up" on the physical needs one has for a lover and best friend.

We began undressing each other slowly, savoring every second. I took her in my arms and placed her in my favorite over-sized chair. There I removed her golden panties and spread her beautifully long legs. I was on my knees in front of her and kissed her toes up to her breasts and up to her lips. Then I spread her legs and licked and licked and licked until she screamed for mercy from the sheer joy of our lovemaking. We moved slowly over to the bed and made love passionately over and over and over for hours.

We arose dreamily and warmed by each other's heat, still clinging madly to each other. We took a long, hot bath in lavender-scented water. Andre, who always attended my suite, delivered a third bottle of champagne and smiled as he sat the bottle down next to the bathtub; he began singing "O Sole Mio" on his way out. We enjoyed the third bottle of champagne while we just luxuriated together under the steaming bubbles. Jill and I laughed and couldn't stop talking about our mutual ecstasy of just being together again and having days ahead to spend together.

Our evening plans included dinner at L'Epee d'Or in Marble Arch, visiting several of our favorite smooth-jazz bars around London, and then going over to Bromley to the "Ramblers Rest" pub for a nightcap before returning to the St. Ermin's. The "Ramblers Rest" usually closed before midnight for the late-night locals, but the owner patronizingly kept it open a little later this evening just for us. This was a special occasion.

Jill and I reveled in the ambience of the old pub and the magnificent fireplace and mantel strewn with RAF memorabilia. As we departed, I left a huge tip for the owner and staff, thanking them for allowing us to relive our past memories and rejoice in our love. They applauded loudly. At thirty-four I am a hopeless Anglophile. Over the years of travel, I had made scores of English friends of both sexes and basked in the closeness and camaraderie of these English friends.

Jill and I returned to the St. Ermin's via private car and fell exhaustedly into bed. Jill went to sleep immediately, but I just sighed and watched her for a long time as she slept before I fell asleep myself. All my expectations of our renewed relationship were met a hundredfold.

Daylight was just peeking around Big Ben, and our first full day was ahead of us. I called down to the St. Ermin's staff, asked for Renee, the early morning staff coordinator, and asked if he could arrange breakfast for us in my suite.

"Of course, Mr. Gilchrist," he said. "The usual—eggs Benedict; petite rib-eye steaks, medium; fresh fruit; croissants; English strawberry preserves; and very hot, strong coffee? And Mr. Gilchrist, should we precede your breakfast with a bottle of Taittinger champagne, sir? It enhances the taste of an early breakfast."

"Yes, of course, Monsieur Renee. You know me well."

After the coffee Jill and I were as excited as schoolchildren on holiday to have a whole day together. Mrs. Hitler was still taking full charge of David and the housekeeping now and was happy for Jill that I was in the picture again. Jill wanted me to see her flat first and then check on our son, David. He was attending a revered private school now and was considered to be an excellent student and an outstanding athlete in soccer and rugby. I had not seen David in eight years. David was ten now, and Jill was ecstatic for me to see him because she said he looked just like me.

24

J ILL GAVE ME an extensive tour of her spacious flat in Bromley
in Kent. The apartment was well appointed, with antiques
and her favorite Impressionists paintings. We stood in the living
room, embraced again, and kissed lovingly for a long time. We
sat down on Jill's Victorian English sofa, and Mrs. Hitler smiled
broadly at me as she served us tea and her fresh homemade black-
currant scones. After Mrs. Hitler left the room, Jill giggled and
told me that Mrs. Hitler only made her fresh black-currant scones
for special occasions.

Then Jill began to tell me about our son, David. She wanted
me to ride with her in her company car to his school and observe
him from a distance. A secretive viewing seemed to be the logical
approach for such a complicated issue. Jill's divorced ex-husband,
the Embassy officer, had been neither a good father to David nor
a good companion for Jill, but she assured me there was never
any violence...only a manipulated, cold distance from David and

an air of formal attachment to her. I didn't ask and couldn't tell if Jill wanted David ever to meet me as his *real* father or not. Maybe secrets were our lives now, mine and hers. I had certainly decided not to reveal to Jill my current lifestyle, my net worth, or how I made my living. The double life I was leading alone might scare her off. Should I be discovered or caught up in a blood feud among the partners, Leo had warned me sternly that the danger to Jill and David could be significant. If I were caught, I would spend decades in jail away from them both, which would drive me mad.

Jill talked on and indicated that she made enough money and had saved enough cash so that if I would stay, money would not be a factor. Jill was still considering my modest salary and commissions from Pan Am. I had mixed emotions about not telling Jill about my actual wealth and the international power I had amassed, but Leo's serious warnings kept me from even being tempted to divulge my finances to Jill. My fortune was now over $450 million after the huge bonus the partners gave me, plus I owned multiple properties around the world that had no financial ties to any government. Canada and Switzerland did not report "off shore" private accounts.

I confided to Jill that money was no longer an issue for me. She was delighted and attributed my new financial independence to the successes I had had from my new promotion to Director of Pan Am World Charters. Jill was generous, and her love for me was exceeded only by her love for our son. Jill was openly anxious for David to have a father who loved them both.

The phone rang, and Jill motioned to me that her car was waiting for us downstairs, off the side lobby. We both went down the back stairs to avoid any prying eyes and to maintain our privacy. I was thrilled and nervous at the same time. I had only seen David as a baby and as a toddler at two, and I was anxious to see the product of my love affair with Jill that had lasted all these years. We drove out of London for about an hour to the exclusive, private boarding school David was attending. Soccer practice was just beginning, and Jill's driver pulled the car, with its dark, tinted windows, very close to the practice field. I picked David out immediately and got a lump in my throat at actually seeing him. At ten years of age, he did look exactly like me when I was his age.

Jill held my hand tightly, and we both wept openly to see him so happy with his peers and at ease with his surroundings. Jill laughed and cried at the same time, telling me that he was surely my son. I was mesmerized and could not take my eyes off him. I took several photos of him with the miniature Leica I had in my coat. He never paid any attention to the limo; the boys were used to seeing them on the private-school campus.

Jill and I stayed and watched David for almost an hour, until the soccer practice was ending. On the way back to London, we held hands firmly, both lost in thought. We entered the St. Ermin's by the side entrance, which went directly into the bar. There I ordered a bourbon and water, chasing my Maker's Mark with a tepid Heineken. Jill had vodka and fresh-squeezed orange juice; she rarely drank more than two drinks. We loved our outing and laughed that we had pulled it off without being caught by our son.

We adjourned to my suite and snuggled together on the hearth in front of the fire. What was she thinking about us and our son? What was the right thing for me to do under the circumstances with the consortium? Wanderlust and adventure still ruled my life, and I didn't think I could be a faithful husband and father at this juncture in my life. I knew, however, that I loved Jill like no other woman...ever.

I asked Jill what she would like to do under the circumstances. We discussed the issues for several hours, and she wanted us to marry and enjoy our son as he grew up and became a young man. She wanted David to have the security of knowing his *real* father and mother were there for him forever. I was concerned about his accepting me after so many years had passed. I had kept up with him only via the verbal updates from Jill. We were both caught in the trap we had created eleven years ago. Yes, our old philanderings had caught up with us.

We laughed and cried over several pipedream solutions to the situation. David's life would change dramatically, as would Jill's and mine. Since David was ten, Jill felt like we should make the major decision soon, but she managed to express her opinion without any pressure or cajoling. There was no easy solution and none without risks. I was most concerned about the triple life I would be trying to lead with a new wife, a soon-to-be teenage son, an executive position with Pan Am, and the demands on my time made by the cartel. The travel alone would be a nightmare, and the pressures from each of those lives would be overwhelming.

Otherwise I thought about continuing my life as it was and moving Jill and our son across the globe to relative safety to my house in Victoria, Canada. Jill would be shocked to learn that she could retire and spend her time with our son and with her leisure activities: writing and painting. Would it be an idealistic dream come true for her or an uncomfortable upheaval in her life? Jill was now fifty-two years old but looked twenty-five. She was in excellent physical condition and good health, and her beauty and attractiveness had only grown over the years. Her slightly silvering blond hair and brilliant-blue eyes were timeless. My central issue was that I had never found another woman like Jill and was so deeply in love with her that none of the other women really mattered. She knew that and felt the same way about me, but now there was David, and David mattered too. I was now thirty-five and holding my age well. I exercised, jogged, and kept in shape, and Jill and I were still hot for each other in and out of bed. Men and women stopped in their tracks when they saw her, as I still did myself. Jill's beauty and her effervescent spirit of joy and happiness were amazing and contagious to all who met her.

I still had to meet with the two remaining partners in Hawaii and informed Jill that I would need to leave for the Hawaiian Islands at the end of our little vacation together. She smiled and said she understood and that we'd work something out over the coming three days. I was so torn as to whether to inform her of my "double employment" and the imminent dangers in my life at every corner. The thought that harm could come to Jill or David because of my complicated risks was unbearable for me. I firmly decided again not to share with her any information about my acquired fortune and power. The dangerous elements of my life would unsettle her and possibly constantly distract her from any genuine happiness she could hope for in a new life with the three of us living as a family. I knew it would be unthinkable to put Jill in a position where she would have to worry constantly about not only her own safety but also about David's.

We spent the next three days revisiting our son's outdoor activities, browsing photographs, and watching home movies of his life during the eight-year period when I was "traveling with Pan Am" as far as Jill knew. These three days were the happiest days of my life. Jill and I made love several times a day and loved being playful with each other around the house, just doing the routine chores of preparing meals and as much housekeeping as Mrs. Hitler would allow. I felt a darkening sense of melancholy creep over me. The three days had passed too quickly, and it was time for me to leave again. After I left, a haunting homesickness settled deep in the core of my being.

25

[JIM HUMMING: "BLUE HAWAII"

BY ELVIS PRESLEY]

F ROM LONDON I took Pan Am to New York then American to
San Francisco to catch up on the Pan American office matters
there. My Pan American boss, the Executive Vice President of
Marketing, commented that our business plan on land arrangements was going very well, and that our charter season would set
new records. Much of the new business was due to Leo and his
staff making land-arrangement recommendations to me throughout Europe. I had done very well hiring new, young, and hungry
charter sales reps, and my judgement calls hiring personnel further impressed my boss and solidified my position as Pan Am's
Director of Luxury Charter Sales, East and West coasts. The increase in sales made my worldwide travel seem even more legit
and credible to Pan American.

I spent several days in the San Francisco house in Walnut
Creek—Jill's house, which she always called "our" house. I caught
up on reading, mail, and bills and then communicated with Leo

regarding the details of meeting the two remaining partners of Inter-World. Leo was pleased with the first two interviews, particularly my interview with Mikos, stating that Mikos had been his close friend and partner for about fifty years.

To release some of the escalating tension, I took out my 1967 GTO 389 and drove the living hell out of her on the freeways around San Fran. It helped me relax, and I always enjoyed driving around the city. Leo cautioned me that the last two partners were close friends and would scrutinize me very carefully individually and also together even though Leo and the other two partners, Demos Mikos in London and Niko Sebastiaan in Amsterdam, had passed me.

I arranged a flight to Honolulu, Hawaii, on Friday to meet the two remaining partners, who were to meet me in Lahaina on Maui. We agreed on two full days of interviewing with casual breaks on both days for socializing and getting to know each other personally. The partners had reserved a deluxe beach villa at one of their luxury resort complexes. I met them early Saturday morning at the consortium's beach villa.

The older partner introduced himself as Li Chang, and the other partner was introduced to me as Mr. Ajit Punjab. They were respectively from Beijing, China, and Mumbai, India, and appeared to be slightly younger than Leo, Demos Mikos, and Niko Sebastiaan. Leo had expanded the worldwide network before and after World War II, while he and the other partners were still very young men.

The meeting with the two remaining partners, Chang and Punjab, was cordial but chilly. With reserved acceptance the last two partners were skeptically contemplating taking into the partnership an American Anglo for the first time. Their trepidations, I presumed, were from fear of exposure or fear of unpleasant years in prison if I were not the right one to take Leo's place. Chang and Punjab had every reason to be extremely prudent. Accepting me as a fifth partner in place of Leo was a very grave decision for them.

Midmorning we ordered a breakfast fit for kings of international commerce—filet mignons, poached eggs with croissants, fresh-squeezed orange juice, a fresh-fruit buffet, pots of aromatic teas, coffee, and a bottle of Taittinger champagne. All was to be served alfresco on the immense porch. The crystal champagne flutes were already filled with fresh strawberries and fresh pineapple. The warm Maui ocean breeze blowing across the wraparound porch of the oceanfront villa was refreshing and welcoming after my cold, severe inquisition by the two savvy Asians. Maui had always been my favorite isle since my Navy duty there over a decade ago now.

During our breakfast the duo continued to grill me on my background even though it was evident they had studied my dossier thoroughly. Leo had added a long list of my accomplishments and had noted that my demeanor during the tensest international business transactions was smartly cool. Leo had also noted as an asset my freedom to travel internationally with a premier airline without being searched. My rapport and reputation were beyond reproach with customs and governmental authorities.

The duo also curiously quizzed me on my acquired private fortune—a subject I quickly closed, asking that it remain private. Nevertheless, they knew already that I had accumulated several hundred million in currency in a number of Leo's "safe" banks in countries which were free from regulation and national taxes. They also knew of my love affair with Jill and at least the number of years we had been close. They did not mention David or Susan Michelle, but their file was very thick, like Leo's, so I assumed they were included.

Mr. Chang and Mr. Punjab both assured me that all of my personal information was kept secret from anyone associated with the conglomerate accept the partners. Mr. Chang and Mr. Punjab made it quite clear that it was extremely important to know every aspect of my life from childhood through my combat experience with the 4th Marines in Vietnam in 1968/69. The two gentlemen indicated that Leo had chosen me as his key candidate due to my global travel experience as well as my extensive combat experience. The two gentlemen were familiar with my military history and decorations and admired my record in the military as well. There is camaraderie among combat soldiers no matter the war. They knew well that I had the strength and skills to stay calm and alert in the most dangerous situation, just as they did.

After long, grueling hours, we adjourned to take a limo ride around the island and discuss the personal casual things men like to talk about: women, wine, song, and travel, but most of all the acquisition of money and power. As we exchanged jokes from our different countries and cultures, their laughs became genuine, and their facades were more relaxed—a refreshing change from their tense personas during the morning at the villa. A solid sense of trust was very slowly beginning to form among the three of us.

The second day was much like the first day, with grueling questions about my views on taking the cartel successfully into the new millennium. Li Chang and Ajit Punjab were seriously blunt about their interests in my plans for the continued success of the cartel. They were anxious to hear what ideas and plans I would put forth. My answer was multifold, diverse consolidation and coordination of the cartel network worldwide. I also put forth my ideas that there were many opportunities outside transporting diamonds and currency. I recommended seeking out real estate opportunities in all of our territories, especially Canada, Asia, and other emerging economies. Additionally I recommended manipulating stock transactions, such as "hedge funds" and other stock opportunities where hundreds of billions, and accumulatively trillions, were within our future reach. Li and Ajit were excited about the unlimited opportunities outside the diamond and currency trade. We all knew that diversification and coordination of financial resources were critical to reach the trillion-dollar goal.

The day was coming to a close. The partners ordered bottles of champagne and trays of hors d'oeuvres and warmly invited me to dine with them. A limo picked us up and took us to a private estate owned by the cartel. There we were surrounded by the most beautiful women I had seen in months. An elegant dinner was followed by more champagne and mingling with the girls, who traveled with and worked for the two Asian partners. All were pros. The evening was magic, and at midnight the partners took me out to the cliff overlooking the ocean. At such a precarious location, I was awaiting my fragile destiny, either to be pushed off the cliff or to be rewarded with their approval. Thankfully they said I had become the fifth partner, with all partners agreeing on my new position. I was to continue to work closely with Leo until he was no longer able to work or make decisions. Their intense concern for Leo's health and their trust in me was finally evident.

I chose several of the Asian girls to join me in my private suite that night; I made love and was professionally loved for hours until dawn. I breakfasted alone late the next morning, absolutely noodled by the frivolous night of playful sex. I was also contemplative over my acceptance as the fifth partner in a multibillion-dollar international conglomerate.

26

[JIM HUMMING: "RUNAROUND
SUE" BY DION DIMUCCI]

P AN AM APPROVED of my setting up a household in London due
to the fact that the majority of our business was in Europe. I
hired a real estate agent to find a suite of rooms in the park area
of London near Bromley in Kent. I could walk in the parks, have
a place to meet Jill while Mrs. Hitler attended David, and maybe
catch glimpses of our son from time to time.

Jill offered me a proposition. She urged me to consider the accumulated savings that she had squirrelled away during her career
years. She had done the math and calculated that we could live on
that amount comfortably for decades. I was amused at how little
she knew about my own personal net worth, which would have
supported us grandly all the way through our senior years. Jill
smiled shyly and said she had never expected me to live without
having other women in my life during my long separations from
her. She said that with my looks, she knew I was bound to have

accumulated a bevy of other women and lovers in my life all over the world. I raised my eyebrows but admitted to nothing.

Jill even offered to let me continue seeing the other women if I would agree to use her house in Bromley in Kent as my primary residence and to be the father figure in our little family when I was in town. Jill knew that my attraction to other women was strong and that my remaining a monogamous lover to her was highly unlikely given my past dalliances. Her love for me was as genuine and unwavering as always. I loved her all the more for that. I must admit, at thirty-seven years old now, my desire to be part of a family was getting stronger, but working toward financial goals was, for now, the stronger enticement and always won out.

The real estate agent found an elegantly furnished suite of rooms for me, which included two private parking places and a conference room I could use for small planning meetings. The London location would enable me to travel to Asia without returning to San Francisco first. The Asian business was continuing to grow exponentially. My itinerary with Pan American and travel plans for the cartel seemed to frequently sync seamlessly, which afforded me great latitude in both businesses. For transportation in London, I shipped my 1967 GTO 389 via Pan Am from San Francisco to London. I was excited at the arrival of my car and drove her all over London and the nearby English countryside. Amazingly I was stopped only once for speeding, which cost me two hundred pounds sterling.

When I arrived back at my suite, my staff members were almost as excited as I was, and all were asking to drive her or at least ride with me somewhere to experience the speed firsthand. The English seemed to love speed and sleek cars. Unexpectedly, I acquired a reputation as local expert on fast cars and attracted the interest of my male and female contemporaries at the Pan American offices as well as my local cartel associates. The candy-apple-red convertible also added more than a few brand-new acquaintances.

The "future-istics" plan, as Niko and I had nicknamed it back in 1980, was my program design for future ventures and lucrative investments that would ensure the future expansion of the cartel's ever-increasing wealth. To the other four partners, I proposed that they send me their top trusted associates from each world region to begin meeting with me to discuss, process, integrate, and finally implement sound plans for the cartel's increasing acquisition of wealth. My first major venture was the cartel's investment in real estate. London was bursting at the seams with possibilities of investment in the growth and development of real estate and land. Real estate was becoming a true asset in almost every country we operated in, and its acquisition required strong political and financial contacts.

For my London headquarters, Pan American provided me with a private corner office in Bromley just a kilometer away from my suite of rooms. I interviewed secretaries for two days before hiring Sarah; also my Pan Am boss in New York City had recommended her. She was a tall, shapely brunette who was single and hot. I wanted some of her right away, and she seemed flirty and more than willing to oblige but only after proving to me that she did indeed have truly exceptional skills as a secretary. Pan American had noted the sharp upward growth in East and West Coast luxury-charter sales under my leadership for the last eight years and in 1983 promoted me to Executive Vice President of world luxury charter sales and land arrangements. The increased salary and incentive package was more than I had expected from them.

Approximately two weeks after I had requested the partners in the cartel to send me their "brightest and best" and most trusted, of course—associates, they began arriving in pairs to join me in London. Sarah, my Pan American executive secretary now, had without questions booked a block of rooms within walking distance of my flat and set up leases in my name for all the rooms for at least a month. Once the entire team arrived, the partners and their associates cocktailed socially for a while and familiarized themselves with one another's expertise and skill sets. Then they went straight into business mode, and I started laying out the specifics of my "future-istics" design, which would ensure the cartel's financial growth for the next decade.

Each of the four senior partners brought diagrams, financial statements, economic tables and indicators, and lists of political allies we had on the payroll in the key cities and provinces around the world where we conducted business. I was astounded by the depth and scope of the cartel's reach into their respective areas of influence, not only in the travel and land arrangements arena but also in most of the future arenas where I wanted to expand the "company."

Among the planning group were five attorneys and their assistants who represented the cartel in each of the geographic arenas where we operated. They astutely interjected any necessary legal issues we might incur as our plans for the future solidified. The attorneys were their own close-knit group and met separately intermittently throughout the month—supposedly, as they joked, to keep us all legal and out of prison. We all appreciated their particular talents toward that end and their contributions to our well-being.

I made daily visits to my Pan Am office to direct Sarah's activities. She was a self-starter and was kept busy providing figures and statistics for projected sales or any other issues the senior Vice Presidents needed, and the statistics they needed always seemed to be required *yesterday*. While we were working one afternoon, Sarah invited me back to her place for drinks. I accepted her invitation knowing exactly where this was headed. I arrived at her well-appointed flat around seven, and she had my favorite Maker's Mark bourbon ready with a Heineken chaser, no less, and a small quiche freshly baked by her and warm from the oven. I could not have been more pleased, and she smiled impishly that her research on me had paid off. I really appreciated her efforts and thanked her.

We sat down on the divan, already in each other's arms, and began heatedly making out almost immediately. We were both hungry for sex and maybe some kinkiness. Sarah had indicated that she liked to experiment with her lovers. She undressed me slowly, saving my silk shorts for last. Sarah knelt in front of me and deftly pulled down my shorts. She began to lick my inner thighs higher and higher until she reached the spot where I thought I would explode. I was on fire, and she continued expertly until she achieved the hot ending she wanted. She knew she was good at this, and indeed she had licked and sucked me as good as any pro I had ever had.

Sarah then led me toward the bedroom for her turn. I picked her up in my arms and roughly laid her down on the king-size bed, where I went down on her as mercilessly as she had done to me. She moaned and screamed over and over, and I enjoyed the power I had over her beautiful, shapely parts. I pushed myself into her, and she arched and begged for more. I showed her no mercy and made wild, uninhibited love to her for hours until we were both wet and satiated. Afterwards, we chatted intimately and lounged luxuriously in the bubbling-hot water of her garden tub.

Now we were both ravenous for treats of a different kind. I was determined that dinner was going to be as spectacular as our earlier evening in bed with each other. I decided to drive us in my own car to L'Epee d'Or, one of my favorite restaurants near Marble Arch. Sarah was excited with the speed at which my GTO 389 convertible could maneuver through London traffic, avoiding taxi traffic and police. The maître d' charmingly seated us at a cozy table and asked us if his staff could bring us anything right away. When I mentioned our order, the staff promptly served us fresh oysters and Taittinger champagne. We laughed at the fun we were both having after the fantastic sex and at how refreshed we felt after the long scented bath and a little champagne and oysters.

The dinner and service were excellent and definitely topped off the evening. Sarah was slightly over six feet tall and was all long, beautiful legs. Her long, flowing brunette hair seemed shiny and alive, and her sense of humor was spontaneous and natural, so rare in stunning beauties. I saw every man in the restaurant eyeing her, and I knew they were jealous. I could feel the heat in my core growing again as she rubbed her leg hard against mine under the table. She gave me a smoldering smile, letting me know she was ready for more.

As we drank a little more champagne, my desire for her overpowered my good sense, and I knew it would be one of those all-nighters where I would leave her flat a little before dawn to go back to my place. The red GTO 389, however, would afford me no secrecy and gave me away as soon as I cranked her up. The garage staff and chambermaids knew exactly who was pulling in, but their years in service had trained them to keep it to themselves.

It had been a wonderfully good night. I had cleared my head of all the tensions of my double life balancing Pan Am and the cartel. The night with Sarah would most likely not be repeated. Sarah had made it very clear that she had multiple lovers and friends who frequently visited overnight. She was smart and savvy and way too appreciative of the outrageous salary I paid her as my Executive Secretary to acknowledge even the slightest change in our relationship at the office. I did, however, call my boss in New York City the next morning and thank him for his recommendation of Sarah for my Executive Secretary. His reply was, "Enjoy."

27

[JIM HUMMING: "YOU ARE THE SUNSHINE
OF MY LIFE" BY STEVIE WONDER]

I ARRIVED BACK AT my suite with little turnaround time after the long, exhilarating night with Sarah. I immediately dressed and prepared for a busy day with the cartel partners and their associates, including the attorneys, who listened silently to every detail and weighed our legal risks at every turn against the clout of our political contacts in every country and probably the cost of buying their legal protection. The business plan we were formulating to ensure the future increasing wealth of the cartel began to take shape. The logistic details were left to the associates, and the scarier details were left to the attorneys, who, as always, promised to try to keep us legal and out of prison. The plan was fundamentally a pyramid structure with the five major partners, including me now, at the top.

$\int$

By 1988 the Inter-World cartel, under my direction, with the detailed consent of the four other partners, had successfully implemented the "future-istics" plan for five years now. The conglomerate had grossed over $2.5 trillion dollars; eclipsing the diamond smuggling and currency manipulations, which were both still very profitable ventures. We maintained the luxury-charter travel business for the convenience of ourselves and our own employees. The luxury-charter sales were actually making such huge profits that we established Trans Galaxy Charters. The cartel now set up its own luxury-charter airlines by investing in several of the Pan American jets and re-branding them as Trans Galaxy Charters. We further expanded our routes and political and legal contacts and employed dozens of new "travel associates."

At forty-two, I am not slowing down but think about it every other day. Maybe the time has come to consider a personal life outside the whirlwind life of Pan American and Inter-World. I had always thought that a "third" life, one with home and family, would be too overwhelming. The indiscretions, philandering, and sexual dalliances in my private life were becoming less of a challenge now. With my very public reputation of wealth, good taste, and "bachelordom", the chase was no longer even necessary. I no longer had to pursue women. The women were doing all of the chasing, all the hard work of the pursuit, and any date I had now was almost assuredly going to land me successfully in bed. The women of my past were blurring together now, and all were too easy and too willing—but not yet boring. Ha!

My future begged for quality that my past lifestyle had not afforded. I now saw clearly the value of the profound love that Jill had for me. Over the past twenty years, her love for me had remained even, pure, and solid despite my sexual adventures with hundreds of faceless and meaningless women whom I had bedded, overlooked, and forgotten. Jill was almost sixty now but as beautiful as ever inside and out. Every past memory I had of her shines brightly in my mind. Jill denied ever being interested in any other man or having any relationship with or any love for any other man besides me, except for our son who was now eighteen. I have literally never had a woman so truly in love with me.

Looking back over the years, I remember flying endless numbers of night skies on Pan Am and looking out of the first-class cabin window into the darkness. I wondered if there really was one woman out there for me whom I could truly love and one could love me back the way I was. Since 1968 Jill had always been there for me, waiting for me for twenty years to come to my senses. I longed for family. I wanted my daughter, Susan Michelle, back in my life, and I wanted to be with my son, David. I wanted to spend time with them, to catch up, and finally to reveal to both of them that I was their *real* dad who really loved them more than life itself. Lost in these thoughts that were driving me crazy, I began humming George Harrison's song "Isn't it a Pity?" where he says we hurt the ones we love and take each other's love for granted.

Passions had driven my life, up to this point, in the wrong direction. It was time for peace. I had flown over a million miles on Pan American and traveled to literally all the major cities around the world. Now all the exotic sexual adventures and international one-nighters seemed to pale in comparison to the quality of love given uniquely to me by a woman I had bedded and fallen in love with twenty years ago. There was no peace within me. I guiltily realized that I *already* had not only the love of my life with Jill but also a family, including a daughter, Susan Michelle, and a son, David, whom I had just lost touch with.

Memories of the restless life I had been leading up to this point put fear in my heart that I would never have the peace and quality of life I wanted unless I made Jill my permanent mate and unless I were somehow able to reconstruct my family, which included Susan Michelle and David. I wanted to follow my instincts now, which were, albeit, slow to kick in.

I called Jill early the next morning and asked her to meet me at the St. Ermin's hotel lobby bar that evening, where we had met so many times in the past. Jill arrived floating beautifully into the room in an emerald-green cocktail dress. She was more than any man deserved. The waitstaff brought my usual fresh oysters and Taittinger champagne without even a nod, and the maître d' had my table in front of the fire waiting. I envisioned our having a few drinks and adjourning to my suite there, and indeed it happened. After making soft, romantic love for hours, we left for a walk in Windsor Park just a few blocks from the hotel. I was tortured in my mind about how exactly to tell Jill that I wanted to marry her and live out our years in Victoria, British Columbia, Canada. We loved both the quaint little city of Victoria and the San Juan Isles in Northern Washington State, where we still had Jill's lovely cottage and gardens in Anacortes. Jill had not even seen my estate and grounds in Victoria.

We walked hand in hand through the Windsor Park gardens and came to rest on a bench there. I held her hand; my eyes were tearing up, and I asked her if she would marry me? She began to sob, whispered a "yes!" and held my hand even tighter. She trembled in my arms as we hugged and kissed passionately and held each other in an even tighter embrace. I've seen her smile that particular smile only once, when I cherished her and made love to her twenty years ago in Kyoto, Japan. Our love seemed to be as peaceful and perfect now as it had been then.

One haunting thought always crept into my brain when I considered marriage, and that was my involvement with the cartel and the threat of attracting danger to my family. Leo had warned me of the possibility of conflict among the other partners over revenue sharing and vying for control of the organization. Leo had stated that a violent disagreement had happened in the cartel fifty years ago, during his tenure as leader. The attempted coup d'état amongst the partners had been quelled with necessary deaths and violence but at the highest cost to himself imaginable. Leo wept as he told me that his beautiful young Greek wife, the love of his life, had been gunned down right in front of him just to prove a point. Again warning me, Leo indicated that having a family and children was a liability and doubly dangerous because of retribution. If a conflict of a serious nature should arise within the cartel, my wife and children would surely be the most effective bargaining chips.

Based on the vast revenues we were now generating, Leo's old warning to me that my family could be put in grave danger of abduction or even death in order to bend me to an aggressor's will seemed even more of a possibility. Leo's warning stayed in the back of my mind every second, and the future I wanted now would necessitate making the safety of my wife and children my constant prayer.

28

[JIM HUMMING: "COULD I HAVE
THIS DANCE FOR THE REST OF MY
LIFE?" BY ANNE MURRAY]

E ARLY THE NEXT morning, to celebrate my proposal and her acceptance, Jill and I went to Tiffany's of London, and I selected, to her delight, the largest diamond surrounded by emeralds that I could conceive fitting on her finger. The executive manager at Tiffany's waited on us himself and knew me by name on sight from my years as a frequent customer who purchased exceptionally expensive jewelry for his lovers, but of course he discreetly did not mention that in front of Jill. After the purchase Jill and I went back to the piano bar and café at the St. Ermin's to celebrate and show off a bit. I requested that Ted, my favorite bartender there, provide "drinks on me." I asked him to open as many bottles of Taittinger champagne as he needed to for his lunchtime crowd.

I was surprised to be congratulated by several of my travel buddies from Pan Am and several from the cartel who had just happened in for lunch. During the morning and through lunch-time, I had spent over a half million dollars on our celebration. Jill was not aware of the expense but was smiling brilliantly to be the recipient of so many congratulatory comments from the imbib-ers. The celebration crowd cheered and toasted us for hours as Jill and I danced for them and kissed passionately. The maître d' even called in a trio to play some of our favorite old songs by Frank Sinatra and Tony Bennett that we had danced to a hundred times before. It was a truly "happening" celebration, and everyone had a ball—at my expense, of course. I gave a very appreciative gratuity to Ted and to the trio who had played for us for hours.

I breathed out, and sighed, and was at peace for the first time in twenty years of wandering and wondering who was out there for me. All along Jill had been there as my best friend, lover, and companion...and had waited for me for twenty years. For the rest of the afternoon, Jill and I adjourned to my suite, and I made the first real, meaningful, and satisfying love of my life.

David was nineteen now, but Mrs. Hitler had stayed on as housekeeper, personal secretary, and cook. Jill called Mrs. Hitler to make arrangements with David's school, Oxford University, and our driver so that our son could join us for dinner. Our car picked David up around four and drove him straight to L'Epee d'Or restaurant to meet us for high tea. David was certainly my son and had sparkling-blue eyes and lush brown hair. His man-ner around us was very confident and congenial, and his conver-sation about an innumerable amount of different subjects was a reflection of both his innate intelligence and his fine education. David was now a freshman and an excellent student at Oxford University, just northwest of London.

I genuinely liked this young man and was a proud papa. We lingered past tea and into dinner and celebrated with the freshest

vegetables, fish, and table wine that could be had. David was surprised at our engagement, but we assured him that it was not done
in haste. We let him know that we had taken it very slowly for
the past twenty years! David sensed his mother's genuine happiness with me, and even at nineteen took the size of the ring on
her finger as an indication that I surely felt the same way about his
mother. I assumed that his fine upbringing and exclusive private-
school manners kept David from mentioning the intervening time
when his mother had been married to the embassy guy. David was
extremely bright and intuitive, so I was sure he had done the math
and realized his mother had been in love with me for a very long
time before and after her superficial marriage. And, to my advantage, David had not bonded with Jake Samples, who had kept a
cool distance from David.

Jill and I had decided to wait until after we were married and
settled to tell David that I was his *real* father. Too much information at one time can be a bad thing. David seemed delighted with
his mother's happiness, and I was hoping that some of his happiness was because he liked me also. The three of us parted company around seven, hugging and kissing all around, and our car was
waiting outside for David to drive him back to Oxford, England,
to his school. David left us with a huge smile on his face. I hoped
that one day I could cause him to smile like that, but his huge
smile this evening was entirely for the happiness of his mother.

My pipedream idea of a happy family seemed more within my
reach than I had ever thought possible, and I sighed again. Jill was
still as excited as a schoolgirl, and the day of drinking and cel-
ebrating had made her even a little giddy. She was anxious to get
back to her house and start contemplating changes and options for
the future, so even though it was quite early for us, we went back
to her home in Bromley in Kent. Jill began working through ideas

concerning her employment and whether she wanted to quit practicing medicine totally or just resign her position in the London area. I was amused by her offering to support us on the money she had set aside the last forty years. She did not know that I had now accumulated over $700 million dollars without tax penalties. Every time I thought about telling her, I froze deep in the thoughts that Leo had put in my head about the mortal danger I could be placing her in.

Jill had loved our time in Victoria and loved Victoria itself. She also thought that Victoria, Canada, would be the perfect place for us to settle down; the Canucks despised the IRS and welcomed wealthy businessmen. I turned in my own resignation to Pan American the very next day. I had trained so many young people well; I knew the airline's international luxury charter business would continue to thrive.

Leo's health had further declined, and he asked me to come again to Cyprus to discuss the details of some final business affairs he wanted me to put in order for him before his demise. He was always the gentleman and expressed genuine interest in my upcoming nuptials. He graciously invited my future bride to come with me and wanted to give us his blessing in person.

Jill surmised quickly that this "Leo" must be a treasured old relative or lifelong friend. She made arrangements for a month's leave before her resignation from International Medical Corps of London became final, so she could joyfully travel with me to Cyprus. She was ecstatic that we were finally able to travel together again, and she had never been to Cyprus. Pan American honorably received my own resignation, and I received appreciative congratulations from all levels.

Leo had one of our own Trans Galaxy jets pick us up at Heathrow airport near London, and we arrived in Cyprus early the next morning. Jill and I retreated to our own suite in Leo's compound, playfully showered together, and took a relaxing nap with the warm, silky Mediterranean breezes blowing across our room. Leo had arranged a dinner for us at noon to celebrate our decision to wed. Leo was obviously dressed by Avilash, who brought him to the table to be with us. Leo himself had traveled to and loved the Victoria, British Columbia, area of Canada and wished us well living there. Leo congratulated me on my resignation from Pan American and seemed sincerely happy for us.

After the meal Avi put Leo back to bed; Jill retired to our suite, and I sat alone by Leo's bedside with Avilash kneeling on the floor nearby. Leo told me privately now that since I had retired from Pan American, he was genuinely relieved that I would stay on with the cartel, since his days were quickly nearing the end. Leo rambled, reminisced, and thanked me for carrying on so well in his absence from the business. He mentioned only a few new items of business he wanted me to keep under my hat for the future of the cartel if I ever needed that particular kind of information. Knowing his time was drawing to a close, Leo had meticulously taken care of a myriad number of other details months ago. We said our good-byes, and Jill and I returned to London late that afternoon.

A month to the day later, Leo passed away quietly in his sleep. Jill and I returned for the funeral and were amazed by the number of employees on the compound and the number of local towns-people and friends who were mourning his death. We attended Leo's funeral in a small Greek Orthodox chapel just outside the compound. The four other partners attended also. We all gathered to pay our respects to the man who had begun it all over sixty years ago with only a thousand drachmas in the pocket of his old, worn-out suit. I was genuinely impressed by the size of the local crowd attending Leo's funeral.

After the formal ceremony, Leo's personal aide, Avilash, in service to him for the past fifty years of his life, handed me a note. Leo had left me a kind personal note of encouragement and warm wishes for my abundant happiness being wedded to Jill. He congratulated me on finally coming to my senses and hoped that my daughter and son would finally be able to bring me as much joy as his daughter had brought him. Of course Leo would know about Susan Michelle and David, but I was puzzled and surprised that he had never mentioned having a daughter himself. I remember Leo had told me years ago that he had selected me because he had no sons. I had certainly met many of the "granddaughters" who lived and worked on the compound, but none of them seemed to be involved in his business affairs, and none seemed to be the caliber that I would expect Leo's daughter to be.

The note from Leo went on to express that he could not have had greater joy watching me "grow up" if I had been his own son. Jill started weeping. Leo stated warmly that I had made him a richer man and that he was able to be at peace during his final days because he knew he was leaving the company he had started in good hands. The note was scrawled in Leo's own fragile handwriting. Jill and I strolled through the gardens on the compound that Leo was so proud of, and both of us wept openly.

29

[JIM HUMMING: "BECAUSE OF

YOU" BY TONY BENNETT]

AFTER THE FUNERAL Jill and I returned to London via Trans Galaxy jet and settled into my familiar suite at the St. Ermin's, ignoring my personal suite of rooms near the office. Dining at the St. Ermin's was so much more delicious and convenient. Since I traveled so frequently, I had never hired a full-time cook and kitchen staff at my London flat. Finally together, Jill and I were so happy. Every hour that Jill was physically close by me seemed to glow with contentment and peace. I had finally realized that Jill had been with me all along in my heart for twenty years.

Since I had already resigned from Pan American luxury-charters sales, Jill just assumed that I was the perfect person to take over Leo's travel business out of respect for his last wishes, and she knew I was the best at travel arrangements. Jill was thrilled that I now had Leo's private airline, Trans Galaxy Charters, at my beck and call too. We began planning our resettlement in Victoria, Canada, and discussing all the details that went along with moving a residence from one country to another. The discussions were the most amicable I had ever had with anyone about a serious topic. It was going to be delightful living with Jill. Why hadn't I gotten to it twenty years earlier?! The "network," as Jill frequently referred to Leo's travel business, Inter-World, was still a highly secret entity for the most part, but they had generously provided us with a coordinator to handle all the details associated with our move from England to Canada.

Our permanent move to Victoria, British Columbia, Canada, was uneventful. We chartered our own private, long-range Trans Galaxy jet to deliver us to Victoria. David, at twenty years old now, was even contemplating moving himself from Oxford University outside London to the University of British Columbia near Victoria, just to be closer to his mother, whom he still thought was his only family. Jill and I planned to live modestly even though I was a very rich man. Jill still insisted on helping out with our expenses, and I allowed it to keep her from wanting to know the extent of my wealth. I set up a secret account with the Bank of Canada and funneled the money that she gave me right back into a private account for her. She never knew of my actions on her behalf. We were both Scottish in our handling of money... The high life I had lived was now a memory in the past.

Jill loved my estate in Victoria, and we enjoyed settling in and having a *home* together again. My estate and the surrounding land in Victoria was quite a step up from the tiny Walnut Creek and Anacortes houses and our flats in the bustling London area. Jill loved having land and being able to spread out and help in the kitchen garden as well as the flower garden. She was as delighted as a child to watch things grow. We both loved strolling around the grounds in the late afternoon after tea and made it a daily routine while a full kitchen staff prepared our dinner.

About four weeks after Leo's funeral, we began planning our wedding to be there in Victoria. Jill had already set up the wedding announcements, and they were being held at an old English print shop in Victoria, waiting for our wedding date to be finalized. We both wanted to work with David's schedule at the University and were anxious for him to attend conveniently. Additionally Jill had established a list of guests, around two hundred, of her medical peers, doctors, friends, nurses, and favorite staff members from the Navy hospitals and from her consulting business at International Medical Corps in London. The wedding was to be held in Victoria at the Christ Church Cathedral, which had a worldwide Anglican membership. Jill and I had visited there and were well received by both the staff and congregation. I invited all of my former Pan American staff members from San Francisco, New York, and London and a few trustworthy associates from Inter-World. All totaled we expected about three hundred guests. I reserved a block of guest rooms at the Empress of China Hotel for our arriving guests at my expense. Most of our guests could use their company expense accounts for their travel and entertainment, and for those whose budgets would be strained, I picked up all of their tabs everywhere, including airfare. Jill had hired a wedding coordinator who was invaluable in perfectly arranging her every wish, and I assigned one of my travel associates to arrange all of the travel, rooms, and local transportation for our guests.

At the estate, Jill had picked a spacious, windowed corner bedroom with a desk, library shelves, and a sitting room overlooking the sound and decorated it especially for David, to be *his* room. I rejoiced at our mutual happiness. David was ecstatic over the wedding and loved our home, which he was already describing to his peers as *his* new home in Victoria. Jill had already purchased

David a dashing tuxedo for the wedding to match my own, and he looked the part of a young executive in the making. Perhaps someday he might take over my position with the organization, as I had done for Leo.

The wedding was spectacular, and everyone who was invited showed up—everyone. The service was exceptionally beautiful, and the Bishop was smiling throughout the vows. The church was adorned with every type of flower one could imagine. Jill particularly liked roses and lilies, and the large sanctuary was filled with the fragrance of these magnificent flowers. Our florist had draped all of the pews and candelabras with hundreds of fresh flowers.

We had the reception at Butchart Gardens, with limos shuttling our guests to the private garden arbors reserved for our celebration. Jill and I hosted over three hundred guests at Butchart Gardens and served only the best food and drink. The menu consisted of fresh Alaskan salmon, filet mignons, grilled pheasant, Dungeness crab claws, fresh oysters, and cheeses from around the world. The late-afternoon alfresco dinner also included scores of fresh vegetables, fresh fruits, and warm breads. There were several open bars in our arbor, and each was stocked with every type of liquor, champagne, wine, and ale to treat every palate. Each guest received a Pacific blue basket that Jill and the wedding coordinator had carefully laden with topnotch champagne, chocolates, dried flowers, and open airline vouchers for each guest and their favorite plus one.

The Victoria skies cooperated, with majestic blue vistas as far as the eye could see. The balmy sea breezes and mild temperatures made our wedding day's weather as near to perfect as one could hope for in the northwest. After tea was served, magnificently crested blue-and-red Butchart Gardens blankets were distributed to those who needed a bit of warming across their laps as they watched the sun set over the Pacific waters of Oak Bay.

The guests were shuttled back to the Empress of China Hotel by limousine to spend the night. They regrouped the next morning in the formal dining room of the hotel for coffees and teas and an elaborate breakfast buffet. The tables were magnificently draped with the roses and lilies from the cathedral, and the buffet offered eggs Benedict, freshly baked warm quiches, an assortment of smoked salmon and cod, fresh fruits, cheeses from all over the world, freshly baked breads that were still warm, and an endless array of pastries and sweets. A large number of small cabana tents were set up on the grounds outside the Empress for the guests who wished to breakfast quietly or privately.

Everyone teased Jill and me about where we would go on our honeymoon, since we both had traveled all over the world. We had to bite our tongues to keep it a secret, but Jill and I had planned to stay on the private estate owned by the "network" in Maui for three weeks. There we could just enjoy each other and start planning our future together. We wanted time to discuss our roles in our new family. We both wanted to focus on David and David's education and on building a strong relationship between him and me. David had already mentioned transferring from Oxford University to the University of British Columbia. We would love that, of course, but wanted the decision to be entirely his.

During the rest of the morning, we managed to wiggle out of great inquisitions as to where we were really going on our honeymoon. As our guests gradually began to leave the Empress of China Hotel, Jill and I stood in a reception line with David, and all of our guests expressed their congratulations and their gratitude for their wonderful weekend away. As they checked out of the Empress of China Hotel in Victoria, we presented each of them with a silver letter opener engraved with "Best Wishes" and our names and wedding date. My private travel agent matched each group of travelers to taxis and limos heading to their various destinations. We had been treated to two days of the bluest skies. In the late morning sun, we said our final good-byes to all of our guests as they left in taxis shuttling them to planes or commuter boats back to Seattle. I thought the wedding was a success.

When our guests had all departed, Jill, David, and I returned to my Victoria estate and were served Campari and soda and a light lunch in the gazebo. We were all three still so happy with the turnout at the wedding. I told David that we were a family now and were looking forward to making future plans with him included as a family member. Jill sat next to David and winked at me that it was time for me to reveal that I was his true father. Jill patted David's hand, and he sensed there was something coming his way. David and I locked eyes, and I spoke slowly.

"David, I've been in love with your mother for twenty-two years, and I am your *real* father. I've never been prouder to say anything in my life."

David was speechless, but he gripped my hand with both of his and smiled broadly. We all three stood up; David gave me a warm, spontaneous bear hug that I immediately returned, and then we all three hugged. Jill teared up with a joyful sense of relief and hopefulness. David was overjoyed and had a lump in his throat as we talked further. He continued to grip my hand as if he never wanted to let go.

We discussed David's education, and I let him know that his financial concerns were over and that I was prepared to send him to any university in the world that he chose. David, himself, brought up the subject that Jill and I were both hoping for. David said that he had already seen his advisor and had started discussing transferring his credits from the Oxford University in London to the University of British Columbia. David confessed that his lifelong daydreams were firstly to know *who* his father was, and secondly he had always wanted to go fishing with his *real* father, like his classmates had done with their fathers.

I added quickly, "David, you are surely my son. I love fishing!" I had loved fishing my whole life and had gone fishing with my father. How could I be *so* blessed to have finally landed not only the love of my life in Jill, but also a son who wanted to go fishing with me?!

In 1990, the year following Leo's death, I was accepted into the cabal as the fifth senior partner in full. My personal net worth was projected to exceed $15 billion dollars over the next decade. The other four partners of Inter-World would also receive like amounts if the forecast for futures in real estate, diamond smuggling, gold exchanges, hedge funds, and stock manipulations around the world were correct. Our projected bottom-line increases were already ahead of schedule, and the partners were rejoicing at their increased wealth due to the success of my "future-istics" business plan around the world.

At forty-four years old, I was blessed with excellent health and was one of the wealthiest men in the world—a fact unknown, of course, to the Associated Press and the international business world. My chosen life in Victoria, Canada, was quiet and sedate, with Jill as my wife and with my son, David, as often as he could get away from college.

At sixty-one Jill also enjoyed excellent health and had taken extremely good care of her body. I had always loved her mind, and she was as quick, bright, and clever as ever. She still turned heads with her beauty and poise wherever we went. When I "came to my senses," as Leo had put it two years ago, I realized that I could not be the person I wanted to be without Jill at my side. She had stood by me regardless of my sexual liaisons with other women around the world, and she had waited faithfully on me even during my long absences from her as I traveled. One of Leo's last requests of me was to stay on as at least the senior advisor to the up-and-coming network's "young Turks." These newer, younger agents needed "squaring up," as Leo had put it. I continued to allow Jill to think that I was flattered that Leo had asked me to continue his *family business*. I was able to pull away from active involvement in Inter-World by following Leo's example. I had a telecommunications expert in "the network" set up a communication center for me here in Victoria, which allowed me to be able to monitor the cartel's major decisions around the world, much like Leo had monitored all the geographics and agents without personally traveling to them. Eventually the network would gross over $40 trillion dollars. As I aged, I became "Leo," the senior advisor for all of the workings of the international enterprises Leo had set up.

Occasionally in my travels, I would come across one of my old girlfriends, and we'd have a drink at an airport lounge or hotel lobby. I no longer had the sexual attraction or passions for these gals which I had had during my younger days. Without exception they offered me their best wishes and recognized how happy I was now. They saw me in love and at peace with the life I had now. The richness of my married relationship with Jill, the "golden" love of my life, had changed my heart forever. I did smile at the memories of my wild adventures with these gals, and they seemed to envy my being relaxed and happy in a situation which they had only longed for and dreamed about.

EPILOGUE

D URING THE FIRST four and a half decades of my life, I lived life to the fullest beyond what I could have imagined, from enduring combat experiences with the Fourth Marines in Vietnam to landing my first job with Pan American Airways to gathering great fortunes, bedding beautiful women, traveling to literally every country in the world, and enjoying every possible pleasure of the flesh. I was still driven to look beyond the present adventure for the next one. I always sought "something" outside pleasures and worldly comforts. Not able to put my finger on the exact object of my dream, I seemed to use these pleasurable accomplishments to temporarily quell my underlying drive to find that missing element.

I satisfied a major portion of that dream by coalescing Jill and David into my family, but like U2's song "I Still Haven't Found What I'm Looking For," the pursuit of adventure always seemed to be ahead of me in my future. Perhaps we all have some portion of that "dream" within us. I pray as I age that perhaps I will secure satisfaction with what I've already accomplished and with the family life that I have established with Jill and David. Perhaps my growing relationship with my son, David, will be the missing piece. I pray that each of my readers will become satisfied with what you have accomplished and with the love that you have given and taken. My elusive dream is still out there, driving me to pursue it.

I have always thought that we should live our lives *sub specie aeternatatis*, or under the aspect of eternity. Jim Gilchrist faces this challenge in the second book, entitled *"Eagle's Flight."* The second of the three books will provide the reader with a higher level of adventure, intrigue, and danger for Jim Gilchrist and his family. Jim Gilchrist is challenged beyond his wildest dreams and will endure grave tragedies if he cannot settle internal rivalries between the partners of Inter-World. Attaining greater fortune and treasure at a price is the focal point of the second book, *"Eagle's Flight."* Jim Gilchrist's charmed life of the past will be turned on end by threats to the lives of the ones he loves and to the destruction of the multitrillion-dollar empire he helped to build. High adventure, dangers, love, and treasure are keys to the second book of Jim Gilchrist's international adventures, *Eagle's Flight*. Enjoy!

ABOUT THE AUTHOR

JIM MCGRAW HAS written the fictitious novel *Sky Diamonds* drawing on episodes and details from his service in Vietnam as a Navy field-medical corpsman and Purple Heart recipient and from his years of international travel as a private luxury-charter salesman for Pan American Airways. Jim is an East Atlanta good ol' Southern boy raised in the Grant Park area and has multiple degrees from Georgia State University.

Jim McGraw is a loving Christian husband to one, father to three, grandfather to three, and brother to two. He presently has a home in Dacula, Georgia, and an estate in Hiawassee, Georgia. Jim has created songs and stories and entertained family and friends for years. Jim is very proud of producing *The R.O.A.D.* in 1997, a thirty-minute film for Georgia Tech and the State of Georgia. Jim wrote the script, raised the money for the production, and created the lyrics and tune that was the opening song of the film. The video was distributed to hundreds of school districts around Georgia and focused on the importance of high-speed Internet to the areas of Georgia outside Atlanta. *The R.O.A.D.* is an acronym for "reach out and develop."

Jim McGraw loves music of all kinds and is always humming something—readers will see the songs he's humming on the chapter headings in *Sky Diamonds*. Now retired and still the entertainer, Jim McGraw is encouraged by all who know him to "write it down" for publication. Enjoy *Sky Diamonds*, the first of three books about the international adventures of Jim Gilchrist, the fictitious character created by Jim McGraw.

Made in the USA
Middletown, DE
20 February 2017